I0728573

PRAISE FOR KAT SIMONS' TIGER SHIFTERS

Once Upon a Tiger

"This is a novel of passion long denied. That banked passion is a flickering flame about to become a raging forest fire. You will be panting yourself before the book ends. […] Readers will enjoy reading this page turner."

—*Night Owl Reviews*

"I really enjoyed this riveting introduction to a new world of tiger shifters with its interesting concepts and bewitching characters. I just with it had been a little longer because it ended way too fast."

—*The Romance Reviews*

"This is the first book in the…series, and I enjoyed it immensely. […] I really want to read the next book of this series to see how Ms. Simons grows this universe."

—*The Romance Studio*

"Victor's backstory broke my heart. What an amazing guy! No wonder Alexis was mad for him […] I was surprised at how much story Ms. Simons was able to fit into so few pages, and I'm hoping this is the start of something bigger. I'd sure like to see more of this crew. Well done!"

—*Long and Short Reviews*

Along Came a Tiger

"…a story with memorable characters and a storyline that keeps you glued to your seat from the beginning to end. […] If you like paranormal romances dealing with shifters then you are going to love Kat [Simons'] Along Came a Tiger."

—*Night Owl Reviews*, TOP PICK

Here There Be Tigers

"The whole book was spellbinding and I was absorbed in the story."

—*Night Owl Reviews*, TOP PICK

Her Tiger to Take

"This is a great read for those like me who want strong characters who feel real and are written in a way that you feel an emotional connection and empathy with as they work to be together."

—*The Romance Reviews*, TOP PICK

To Tempt a Tiger

"I definitely want to stay involved in this world and visit more of the couples and their friends and family."

—*The Romance Reviews*, TOP PICK

Down Will Come Tiger

"The chemistry is a smoldering inferno of heat but this relationship is slow burning because of personal demons and emotional distress and these strong, compelling characters draw readers in and capture their hearts…The well written scenes and details capture the imagination and bring the story to life while the intriguing events keep readers glued to the pages."

—Night Owl Reviews

TITLES BY KAT SIMONS

Tiger Shifters Series

ONCE UPON A TIGER
ALONG CAME A TIGER
HERE THERE BE TIGERS
HER TIGER TO TAKE
TO TEMPT A TIGER
DOWN WILL COME TIGER

ONCE UPON A TIGER

Tiger Shifters

KAT SIMONS

ONCE UPON A TIGER

Copyright © 2013 by Katrina Tipton
All rights reserved.

Published 2013 by T&D Publishing

Cover art design © 2013 and 2016 The Killion Group

Interior book design © 2016 T&D Publishing

ISBN-13: 978-1-944600-00-6 (Trade Paperback edition)

This book is licensed for your personal enjoyment only. All rights
reserved. No part of this book may be reproduced, scanned, or distributed
in any print or electronic form without written permission from the author,
excepting brief quotes used in the context of a review.

This is a work of fiction. All of the characters, places, organizations,
and events portrayed are either products of the author's imagination or
are used fictitiously. Any resemblance to actual persons, living or dead,
business establishments, events, or locales is entirely coincidental.

First printing: March 2016

For information, contact T&D Publishing: www.TandDPublishing.com

To my family. Just because.

ACKNOWLEDGMENTS

I owe a lot of people many thanks for their help in getting this book out. I want to thank my husband for calming me when I wanted to go nuts, and my boys for occasionally giving me time to work (even if it was only occasionally). This wouldn't be happening now if not for my fabulous friend, Louise Fury. Thanks for pushing me to do this! I'd also like to thank Kem Shortland for all her help with editing and formatting questions. You are a star! And a huge thank you to Kim Killion for the beautiful cover art she made for me. Finally, I'd like to thank some other dear friends for their support: Hope Tarr, Elizabeth K. Mahon, Mala Bhattacharjee, Leanna Renee Hieber, Stacey Agdern, Lise Horton, and Cassandra Carr. Thanks, ladies, for everything! Finally, I'd like to thank my parents because they keep believing in me even when I stop.

ONCE UPON A TIGER

Tiger Shifters

KAT SIMONS

CHAPTER ONE

"Idiots." Alexis Tarasova growled low in her throat at the scent of five…no six male tigers invading her territory. She couldn't tell who they were yet, but in her current state, their presence set off deep instincts.

Angry instincts.

This was her space. No males were allowed here without her permission. And she had not given it. She didn't give a damn she was in estrous or that her body was a raw bundle of need and lust. She *didn't* run and wasn't going to be forced into it by anyone.

If she had to beat the lot of them into bloody pulps to make her point, she would.

She stood in her human form on the front porch of her small Catskills cabin and folded her arms across her chest, staring into the trees. Despite the full moon shedding light into the clearing in front of her home, the woods beyond were pitch black. She was surrounded by the orange, gold, and red leaves that made this area of New York so beautiful this time of year, but only shades of grey and black were visible now. If she were an ordinary human, she wouldn't have been able to see much of anything beneath the trees. In tiger form, she'd see well into that darkness.

She didn't bother stripping off her loose jeans and flannel shirt to make shifting easier, though. She would face them in her human form to make a point. After twelve years working as a Tracker—the only female Tracker—she didn't need to be a tiger to take them on. She'd been trained by her uncle to be the most deadly of the elite enforcers of Tiger Law. She'd dedicated most of her life to upholding her peoples' rules, hunting down dangerous tigers, killing when necessary. No one forced her to do anything—not even the Mate Run.

The males were approaching fast, but carefully. She heard them now. They weren't making any attempt to hide their presence. Her quiet growl drifted out on the still air.

Alexis wasn't opposed to the mating ritual on principle. The Run had saved her people from self-destruction. The female birth rates had dropped so significantly two centuries ago it had left them on the brink of extinction. Out of desperation, the males had started fighting too much, and raping—sometimes killing—the females. The situation grew increasingly worse until the elders, the leaders of her people, instigated a new law.

During estrous, a female ran from a group of males, allowing one to catch her and spend that cycle with her. The couple had as much sex as possible during those three days.

If she got pregnant, they were allowed to be mated—either permanently marry or be together for as long as they wanted. If she didn't get pregnant, she had to run again. The tigress could choose the same male or a different male, but until she got pregnant, she kept running.

The ritual had saved Alexis' people. No more gang rapes, no more death-match challenges amongst the males. The female birth rates were still extremely low, her people were still on the very edge of extinction and searching for some way to survive, but at least they weren't making things worse anymore.

But she was a Tracker. An enforcer of her peoples' laws. She required a level of fear and respect from the other tigers in order to do her job. And having to run from any of them was contrary to every instinct she had, even if she got to choose who caught her.

She didn't run. She fought. She wasn't chased. She did the chasing.

The elders had supported her decision to forgo mating. Why these males thought they could overrule their governing body and force this on her, she didn't know. She didn't really care. She had no intention of giving in to the pressure.

If she got pregnant, the entire point of the Mate Run, she'd be forced to give up her job. Not something she was ready to do, and might never be ready for because the only man she could see having a family with wasn't allowed to mate.

She released a soft breath and tried pushing the ridiculous longing she felt for Victor Romanov to the back of her mind. She couldn't have him. And no one else had ever come close to capturing her interest. She'd wanted him for years, but they weren't meant to be. That made forgoing the Run easy.

She forced herself to focus on her anger and those stupid fucks stalking through her land. Being distracted now would only get her hurt. A cool autumn breeze brought her the rich smells the surrounding woods, the moist dirt, the sweet, pungent detritus, the earthy mix of beech, maple, and a hint of pine bark, the faint tang of the few small mammals brave enough to frequent her territory…and the sharp bite of male tiger musk.

Her lip curled.

When she sensed them nearing, she let her growl carry into the trees, a warning and a challenge. Two of the five answered with soft chuffing noises. Frowning, she studied the darkness. Five. But she was sure there were six. Where was he now?

She let her senses stretch, trying to find that sixth, but the appearance of the others divided her attention. Three Siberian tigers and two Bengals stepped from the woods, forming a semi-circle around the front of her home. She narrowed her eyes and let their scent-signatures come to her, trying to identify them. Each had a unique combination of feline musk and the complex weave of pheromones that were impossible to put into human words. If pushed, she'd describe them as a kind of individualized spice mixture, but some of the "spices" didn't actually exist.

She knew two of the invaders.

One Siberian, Nick Jameson, was a fellow Tracker and until this moment she would have considered him a friend of sorts. At the least, a respected colleague. She was more than a little surprised he was a part of all this, as he'd never shown any particular interest in her—not any more interest than he showed any other female.

The second, a Bengal named Dev Gupta, was another story. He'd been pestering her for the last two years. Despite her rebukes, he'd continued hitting on her, once getting so aggressive she'd had to dislocate his shoulder to make her point clear. He hadn't been nearly as forward since, but she wasn't shocked to see him.

She studied the other three and thought she might recognize another of the Siberians. He seemed vaguely familiar. She encountered a lot of tigers during the course of her job, especially at the elders' U.S. compound in West Virginia. As the seat of her people's government here in the States, the compound saw a steady stream of tigers in and out for audiences with the elders or to deal with political and legal issues. She could have met him there at some point, but she couldn't put a human face or a name to him.

The remaining two were strangers to her, so she made sure to memorize their unique scent-signatures. She held each of their gazes in turn, letting them see her anger, her irritation, her complete lack of fear. She let another soft growl fill the air.

The woods fell silent. The air went still and cold. Alexis matched the quiet of her surroundings—a dangerous predator waiting for her opponent to blink first.

Finally, Nick stepped forward and shifted. She kept her attention on the group as she waited for him to finish. The process took only a few minutes, which was a sign of a strong male. She made note, filing the fact away for use in the fight she knew was coming.

"Alex," Nick said when he straightened to his full height.

He was over six feet tall with shaggy brown hair and dark blue eyes. He was muscular, a trained fighter, not a tiger to be taken lightly.

"Nick. You have some explaining to do." As soon as she said the words, a silly part of her wanted to say the line again with a strong Cuban accent, an imitation of Desi Arnaz's oft-repeated line in *I Love Lucy*, but she resisted the impulse. This wasn't a moment for her odd humor.

"You know why we're here," Nick said.

"You know I don't run."

"You've had your little rebellion, Alex."

She raised her brows at his condescension but didn't comment otherwise.

"What makes you exempt from this rule of our people?" he asked. "There aren't enough females for you to be allowed to forgo mating."

"I. Never. Run."

Despite her insistence, her hormones were high, her skin alive with sensation. Tingles of unfocused lust skittered along her nerves, sharper for her anger. The presence of so many ready males made things worse. She wasn't a slave to her reproductive cycle, but it did make her *want* in a way that could be hard to control. The call to mate always left her edgy and irritable. Usually, she escaped the need by picking up a human

man and taking him to bed for three days. But years of this got old, and all she wanted now was to wallow in her own territory, alone, until the desperation passed.

"No female is allowed to skip the Run," Nick said, taking two steps closer to her porch. The tigers behind him shifted quietly, low grunts and growls greeting his comment. There was a bristling of fur, a slight adjusting of stance.

Alexis took in their positions and sizes, automatically preparing strategies, both defensive and offensive. The cool air brushed her skin as her senses heightened. She unfolded her arms and let them hang at her sides, loose and ready. Then she held Nick's gaze as she repeated, very distinctly, "I don't run."

The tigers surged forward. Alexis braced for the attack, then sensed the sixth tiger, the one she'd lost track of, coming up on the left from behind her cabin. She cursed, half-turned to face the new threat, and the sixth tiger, a blur of orange, white and black stripes, leapt into the clearing between her and the others.

Facing the others.

Everyone froze. Alexis blinked several times as she took in the fact that this newcomer was standing between her and the males. A moment later, she caught his scent.

Victor Romanov.

Her heartbeat quickened. A combination of panic, shock, and need tightened like a band around her chest. The one man she was susceptible to, the only one she'd ever wanted…

What was he *doing* here? Especially now, when the call to mate rode her so hard she could barely resist the urge to drag him inside. How could she focus, how could she fight the others with Victor such a powerful distraction?

She gritted her teeth and worked on slowing her pulse. She would question him later. Right now, she had to deal with the more immediate threat.

Nick, still in human form, stared at him. "Victor," he said quietly. "This isn't your fight. She has to run. The elders have said she's no longer allowed to avoid her duty to her people."

That was news to Alexis and enough of a shock to distract her from having Victor so near.

"What? Elizaveta would never agree to that." Elizaveta Chernikova, the only female elder, was also her sponsor as a Tracker. And the closest thing she had to a mother since her parents' death.

"She was a dissenting voice," Nick allowed. "But she was outvoted. You've avoided the Run for too long. Our people need you."

"I serve our people. As a Tracker."

"We need you to reproduce now."

"I'm not just some walking womb," she growled, her anger making the hair on her neck and arms stand up. She stepped to the edge of her porch. "There are other females. Find them and be happy. But I *will not run*."

The four still in tiger form started stalking forward again. Victor lowered slightly on his haunches, preparing to leap. His silence was eerie amidst the other chuffs and low growls. The approaching tigers hesitated. Where their hormones made them brave with her, their instincts didn't completely leave them when faced with Victor's heavy silence.

She smiled at Nick. "I could take you all on my own. You know that. I've earned my reputation honestly." She glanced down at Victor, then back at Nick. "But do you really want to face us both?"

"He's damaged, defective. He's not allowed to have you," Nick spat. "He's not allowed to run."

"If you want a fight, you'll get one, but I will not be coerced into mating. No matter what the elders say." She looked him over. "You shouldn't have pushed this, Nick. If I ever do decide I want a mate, you won't even be considered."

"We'll see about that."

He flashed her a smile she might have found attractive, even sexy, if she wasn't so infuriated. But she wasn't interested in Nick so just stared at him without reacting, waiting for him to decide his own fate.

The confident tilt of his mouth dropped into a slight frown. He glanced at Victor again, then back at her. Finally, he made a grunting noise and turned back toward the woods. The other tigers hesitated and then joined him, disappearing into the dark.

She waited for long moments, listening to their retreat. They went far enough that she could no longer sense or smell them. But she had no illusions they'd left for good. This was only the first day of her estrous. She had another two days to get through. If Nick was telling the truth and the elders had really given the males permission to force her into a run, she knew those two days wouldn't be the quiet holiday she'd hoped for.

"Fucking Mate Run," she muttered. Then looked at Victor.

He had turned toward her and sat patiently watching her. He was a beautiful tiger, his thick orange fur and black stripes lovely in the moonlight, his dark eyes large and serious. As a human, he was just as handsome and compelling. Something she was trying not to consider or think about.

She failed. She couldn't stop imagining what he'd look like after he shifted, when he'd be beautifully nude and so deliciously close. This was only the second time she'd seen his tiger form, and she'd never been around when he shifted, so she'd never had the pleasure of seeing him without clothes. Right now, it was all she could think about. Her body pulsed with need, and every cell was focused on *him*. She'd resisted her attraction to him for so long. Years of denial were coming back to bite her on the ass. Her defenses were down, and having him here was trouble.

His full focus was on her, the attention giving her little shivers of awareness. Her stomach tightened as heat crawled through her body. She clenched her thigh muscles in an attempt to calm the rising ache between her legs. Damn it. He was the one tiger who could upend her every defense. Why the hell was he here?

She swallowed down the thick longing and forced herself to think.

They had to talk. He'd be able to tell her if the elders really had decided to force her to run. She was anxious to find out why he was here, too, when being around her during her estrous was so potentially dangerous.

Talking with Victor required something for him to write with, though. He was mute, not deaf. There'd been an attack of some kind when he was four, though she'd never talked with him about the details. Of all the stories about him, she wasn't even sure which were true. All she knew was that he hadn't spoken since the attack, so he only communicated with her in writing.

She could use the sign language she'd been secretly practicing for years. She'd seen him signing with his mother a couple of times and once with another male. He rarely signed in public, but knowing he could was enough to get her started on studying the language. She'd never actually used it with anyone, though, so she wasn't sure if she'd be able to carry on a real conversation with Victor.

Which brought her to another worry. She had no idea how he'd feel about her signing with him. He seemed to use it so infrequently. Would he consider it an invasion of his privacy or maybe too personal if she just started signing with him? Admitting she could sign might give away her obsession with him. The idea of revealing that much left her feeling surprisingly shy and insecure. She didn't know how Victor felt about her. Revealing her feelings now, when her estrous left her so vulnerable…

No. She wasn't ready for the degree of intimacy signing would imply. Not yet. Maybe not ever.

She gestured to his huge paws. "You might as well shift so we can talk. Can't write with those. I think I have a pad and pen inside."

She went back into her home, giving him privacy to change, and herself a few minutes to calm her speeding heartbeat.

CHAPTER TWO

To Alexis' surprise, Victor was standing at her door only a few minutes later. She swallowed and tried not to stare. He was magnificent, muscled and lean, with just the right amount of hair covering his human body. The hard cut angles of his face should have made him look harsh but somehow he just looked more compelling. Black eyes, closely cut dark hair, and a sexy half-smile that made her stomach muscles tighten, all combined to send her heartbeat pounding.

She'd never been around Victor when she was in estrous. In fact, since coming to terms with the knowledge that her obsession with him could never lead to a future, she'd made an effort to never spend time alone with him. He was the head security technician at the elders' compound, so they crossed paths regularly. But she tried making sure there were others around to keep her from doing something stupid.

Unfortunately, she hadn't always been successful.

She flashed on a recent memory of literally bumping into him in a corridor at the compound when she'd been too deep in thought to notice her surroundings. He'd held her arms while she caught her balance. The contact sent shivers of desire shooting through her body, forcing her to step back as soon as she could, then apologized.

He pulled a notebook from the back pocket of his dark jeans and wrote, *You okay?*

"Fine. The job I'm heading out on has me…" She shrugged. "It's a tough one."

A friend?

"No. Nothing like that." She made the mistake of looking up to finish and got momentarily caught in the deep darkness of his steady gaze. Her stomach danced in giddy delight even as her heart tightened. Swallowing, she said, "The tiger I'm going after has something wrong with him. He's started stalking children."

Human or tiger?

"Human."

Dangerous.

"Exactly." Dangerous to their people if he were discovered by the humans. Also dangerous for her as her target couldn't possibly be sane if he was hunting kids.

Has he hurt any yet?

"No. Fortunately. He came close twice, though. I have to find him soon."

Do you want help?

She straightened. No one offered to help her. Not since she'd taken the Tracker oath. But he looked serious. And beneath the façade he normally wore, she sensed a hard core of intensity only a stupid person would challenge. His silence was intimidating enough, but for the first time, she saw a dangerous edge to him.

And he was offering to help her. The gesture touched her in ways she wouldn't have expected. Suddenly, she was aware of just how alone they were and just how desperately she wanted him.

"I'll be fine." Even as she said this, her heartbeat quickened and she had trouble speaking above a whisper.

I know. But if you need me, I'm here.

Her pulse pounded loud in her ears as she read. Could he hear it? Did he realize just how much she needed him—just not for the hunt? She found herself staring at his mouth. The urge to lean in and taste him overwhelmed her.

Alexis blinked back the memory and realized she was once again staring at Victor's mouth. This time, there was no one around to interrupt them and keep her from giving in to the years of wanting. During that previous meeting, a member of his security tech team had required his attention and he'd hurried away, leaving her breathless. She'd brought in the rogue tiger with a little more aggression than she might have normally. And then she'd taken herself off to her retreat here in the mountains to wallow in the frustration of having to resist the only man she wanted.

Now Victor was here. No one between them. And her hormones were making things infinitely worse.

His being naked did *not* help her control either—which was hanging on by a very tiny, thin thread.

She motioned to her bedroom. "I'm sure I've got something in there big enough to fit you." She generally kept a few spare things on hand for the Chernikov brothers, the only males allowed in her territory. Victor would fit into the oldest boy's clothes.

He nodded and strolled easily through her small living room to the large bedroom that took up the left side of her cabin.

To keep from staring at his ass, she turned to the fireplace and stoked the flames. They didn't need the heat. It wasn't all that chilly—especially for her kind, with their high metabolisms—but she didn't like using her generator in the evening when she didn't need it, so the fire was the only light in the room. Any light was better than being in the dark with Victor. Darkness forgave mistakes. In the dark, it was easy to pretend she could have him. If she allowed herself any room to act, she'd follow him into her bedroom and take advantage of his nakedness.

He was forbidden by the elders from taking a mate, though. And she was in estrous. If she fucked him now, she risked getting pregnant—and bringing down the wrath of the elders on them both.

She stared at her open bedroom door. She couldn't do that to him. Or rather, she didn't want to do that to him. Right now, it was hard for her to think beyond the need to have him.

Why the hell was he here?

She pulled in a deep breath in an attempt to calm her racing heartbeat only to get hit with his distinct and delicious scent. Damn but the man smelled good. Musk, male, a hint of something earthy, and that impossible to describe mix of pheromonal "spices" that flavored her tongue and infused her senses.

She was so much more sensitive to him right now. Damn it. Why, why, why was he here?

Her acutely sensitive ears picked up the sound of material slipping over his body as he got dressed. Oh, that was too much to deal with. She went to a nearby table, snatched out a pen, then went hunting for some paper. She finally found an old notebook tucked in between her collection of paperbacks on the bookshelf outside her bedroom door.

Victor walked out just as she recovered the pad, so she shoved it and the pen into his hands and turned her back on him. He wore a pair of cargo pants and a flannel shirt. He was about the sexiest looking man she'd ever seen. Clenching her jaw to keep from jumping him, she hurried to the open kitchen on the opposite side of the living room.

"You want something to drink?" She made a face when she realized he couldn't answer if she wasn't looking at him, then looked over her shoulder.

He smiled and nodded.

"Beer?"

He shook his head.

"Water? The only thing I have besides water is diet soda. And tea. But I'll have to boil the kettle."

He flipped open the notebook, jotted down something and crossed to show her his answer.

"Water it is, then," she said. It was embarrassing how fast she rushed away from him.

She stayed quiet while she got his drink, coming to terms with the fact that she was going to have to sit close to him so they could communicate. Her eyesight was good, but she couldn't read his notes from all the way across the room without it being awkward. And obvious.

Blowing out a breath, she faced him and gestured to the couch. He sat and accepted the glass. She stood for a minute too long before finally settling next to him.

"Okay. Why are you here?" She asked the question she'd been repeatedly asking herself. "If it's because the elders have said I have to run…" She trailed off, leaving an underlying threat unspoken, because she couldn't bring herself to tell him an outright lie—that she wouldn't give in to him either. She would, if he pushed. But she still had no intention of running, so her threat wasn't entirely hollow.

He smiled, slow and sexy, then set the water aside, and wrote, *I'm not allowed to run.*

She frowned. She knew that. It didn't mean he wouldn't try something. And he might have if he was any other tiger. But this was Victor. Controlled, self-contained, mysterious and so, so hard to resist.

"Fine. Then why are you here?"

I thought you might need help.

Again offering her help. A warm, soft feeling suffused her. "You knew they'd try to make me run?"

As soon as the elders told Nick you weren't allowed to avoid it any longer.

"It's true then? They really said I have to run?"

He nodded.

"So, they basically sicced Nick on me? Rather than send someone I might trust to let me know, they sent a group of males to force the Run on me without the decency of warning me?"

They did think you'd trust Nick since he's a Tracker. I got the impression they were afraid you'd go into hiding and not even give the Run a chance if you were warned before your estrous.

"Bastards. After all I've done for them. All the years of service. The only thing I ever asked in return was immunity from the Run." She met Victor's steady gaze. "Do you think I'm being selfish, avoiding mating?"

It's not my place to say. You should be allowed to live as you like.

She snorted a sound that wasn't quite a laugh. "Tell that to the rest of our people."

The elders' decision that she must run now meant she was going to end up fighting tigers she would otherwise have gotten along with. She might even have to kill some of them to protect herself. Where would that leave her?

She blinked and focused on Victor. He was staring at her as if he could see into her thoughts.

"If I have to kill any of them, because the elders have said I have to run, does that mean I'll become a criminal?"

Victor nodded.

Anger rose to heat her skin. Damn the elders. They were boxing her into a corner. They had to know she'd fight—even if she'd wanted to mate with any of the males they sent after her. Why do that to her?

She tilted her head. Victor's presence took on a whole new meaning.

"Is that why you're here? To keep me from killing them?"

He smiled and dipped his head again.

She laughed, a short burst of emotion at the absurd situation. "Bet Nick doesn't know he should be thanking you."

Victor shrugged.

"But you weren't facing me, keeping me from going after them. You were facing the others."

They were the ones trying to start a fight.

"True." She leaned back against the armrest. "So now what? I know they haven't gone away. It couldn't be that easy."

I'll stay. To help.

She worked at squashing the rapid increase in her pulse, but from the way his nostrils flared and his eyes narrowed slightly, she knew the effort was pointless. He could smell her lust rising. And there was no way they'd be able to remain this close without falling into bed. She'd wanted him too much for too long. Even out of estrous, she'd barely been able to resist him. Alone with him, she knew her body would get the better of her brain.

Just the thought made her glance toward her room. When she looked at Victor again, his expression was serious, his gaze focused on her mouth.

"That's probably not a great idea," she murmured, even as she leaned a little closer. "Not while I'm in estrous."

She felt his heat, smelled his desire. The combination was driving her nuts. Every fiber of her being strained toward him, wanting to strip off those borrowed clothes and do all sorts of naughty things to his delicious body. When she realized just how close she'd gotten to him, she jumped up and stumbled back toward the kitchen.

"No," she said once she was at a safe distance. "No, you hanging around is not a good idea."

He dropped eye contact long enough to write a note, then rose slowly, his every movement holding her attention. So graceful and strong. What would those big hands feel like on her body? Her skin quivered at the thought. She closed her eyes for a moment to rein in her wayward thoughts. When she opened them, he was standing in front of her, holding the notebook up so she could read.

I won't stay here. I'll keep to the woods. But I'll be near enough to help if you need me.

She didn't want him to go. She wanted him to stay, to drag her off to bed and fuck her like there were no consequences or repercussions. She could barely think around the thick need racing across her heated skin, the only relief for it in Victor's arms.

He dropped his hands to his side and took a small step closer. Alexis was so overwhelmed by him she stopped thinking. To hell with the elders and their damned rules. She eased near enough that their clothes brushed. She felt the contact across her entire body. Her nipples hardened, her breathing increased, dampness soaked her underwear.

Their mouths were a breath away, the suspense and desire almost more than she could take.

Then she blinked and he was gone.

An involuntary gasp blew past her tingling lips. She stood exactly where she was for long moments as she concentrated on breathing. Finally, she went to her still-open front door. There was no sign of him. But her keen senses picked him up about a half mile away. Far enough that she was no longer so driven to drag him to bed but close enough he could reach her if she needed him.

True to his word, she thought. Honorable on top of everything else.

No wondered she'd been in love with him for most of her adult life.

CHAPTER THREE

Victor paced the woods in his tiger form, his senses open so he would know if the other males entered Alexis' territory again. It was harder to resist going to her while he was tiger, but he was also faster, stronger, and more deadly in this shape.

Exactly what she needed from him right now.

He turned in the direction of her cabin and scented the air. She called to him. Not on purpose, he knew. Now, more than any other time, she was a beacon to his desire, a bright white light in the blackness. She drove him wild, past even his usual obsession with her. He was a fool to think he'd be able to stay away.

Yet he couldn't leave her to face the others on her own. She was perfectly capable of taking care of herself. Just a few months ago, she'd brought an unbalanced tiger in to face the elders' justice without any help—a tiger whose insanity made him infinitely more dangerous than the current threat. She was an efficient and deadly Tracker.

But this was different. The elders hadn't even warned Alexis they'd changed their minds about her not running. Now that she was being forced to mate, it would kill him if something happened to her when he could have helped. His own weak will, his inability to resist her, wasn't an acceptable reason to stay away.

So he continued stalking through the trees, the soil and dead leaves a steadying cushion beneath his paws. Autumn was crisp in the night air. He tried focusing on the scents and sensations of his favorite season—the pine and maple, the earthy scent of dying leaves, the moist soil. But underneath it all, Alexis' scent rose up to tease him—a feminine musk woven with hints of cinnamon and allspice, along with those unique pheromone flavors he'd never found human words for. This was her territory. There was nowhere for him to go that wouldn't carry her essence.

If he were smarter, he'd leave. There was no telling what punishment the elders would inflict on him if he gave in to his need for Alexis. He was forbidden a mate. "Defective" males couldn't be allowed to reproduce with the few remaining females and risk producing defective offspring. That was the argument anyway.

He might have fought the decree. He wasn't mute because he chose to be—a mental defect as far as the others were concerned—he was mute because of a physical injury. The only woman he'd ever wanted refused to run anyway, so he'd never cared that they excluded him.

Now… Well, that was another reason he'd come to guard her back. He wanted to gauge her reaction to the news, to see if she was ready to take a mate. If she was, he'd have to give up any illusions she might be his one day. He wasn't allowed to have her, but as long as she didn't run, he could pretend.

His relief at her reaction to the other males was selfish. Her resistance, the way she showed no interest even in Nick, was more than a little satisfying. Part of him, his tiger he supposed, insisted she was his. That part didn't want to listen to logic or rules or conventions of his human self. He just wanted to take her and make her his.

Turning toward her cabin again, he felt the coming dawn ruffle through his fur and wondered what she was doing.

Less than half an hour later, she walked toward him through the trees, a magnificent Siberian tiger. Light from the rising sun glinted in her coat. He actually forgot to breathe as he watched her stalk near. When he remembered, his indrawn breath pulled her scent into his mouth, coating his tongue with her taste. He swallowed that delicious flavor as his heartbeat sped. His claws dug into the soil and his tail swished sharply. He couldn't get enough of her. And seeing her in the pink light of dawn made him forget why he was here.

She nudged his neck, making a soft chuffing noise, then trotted back a few steps and faced into the woods. He stood perfectly still. She couldn't want him to chase her. He was absolutely positive she would never run from any male, even this deep into her estrous. But then what did she want?

She repeated the neck nudge and the little trot away and he finally understood. She did want to run, but she wasn't asking to be chased.

They took off together, running faster than a normal tiger could, weaving around the trees, remaining level with each other. The release of tension swamped him with joy. Running at her side was a kind of pain and ecstasy he would hold onto for the rest of his life. He had to work to keep up with her, which thrilled him further. No lightweight, his Alexis. She was everything strong and magnificent about a tigress.

She raced beside him, her lithe form elegant, the deep orange and black stripes of her coat glistening in the morning light, her muscles bunching in sensual ease. Her scent filled him and his nostrils flared to pull in more. His body demanded he move closer, rub against her, mark her, claim her as his. He ducked his head and edged in as close as he dared, a touch of danger adding punch and excitement to the run. She could turn on him and attack if she felt threatened, so he was careful to resist anything overtly territorial. But his cat wanted her so desperately, he would have roared if he could.

They ran over the early autumn detritus, circling her territory. As they did, he noted the other males keeping their distance several miles outside of the perimeter. They hadn't left the area as he'd suspected. He knew they'd return, but for the moment, they weren't an immediate threat.

He let Alexis choose their direction, following without chasing, but he was still surprised when she brought him back to her cabin. The sun was hanging higher in the sky. It wasn't safe to be in tiger form anymore, even though her cabin was in an extremely isolated part of northern Ulster County. Chances of being seen by random hikers or hunters rose during the day so most tigers kept to their human forms.

She padded onto her porch and into her cabin without pausing. He remained in the clearing, not sure she'd welcome him in again after what almost happened last night. He did need to shift, though, and his pack with his clothes—including the clothes he'd already borrowed from her—was over a mile away. He should return to his camping spot and leave her be. The morning exercise would have to be enough. But as he turned to leave, she came back out of the cabin in human form, a robe covering her nude body—a small mercy for his poor heart.

Though the robe did nothing to stop his imagination. He couldn't help staring. Her short dark hair was a sexy, tousled mess, her blue eyes electric against the morning light, her broad features relaxed, her expression almost sleepy. She was long and lean, even in human form, but had exactly the right amount of curves to take his breath away. He wanted to strip the silky material off her more than he wanted to see his next sunrise.

"Come in, Victor," she said. "Have breakfast with me. I'd like to try talking some more."

Her wry smile tugged at his lust. Talk. Right. That's what he wanted to do right now. Sarcasm edged his inner voice.

"For as long as we can manage," she said. "There are clothes in the bathroom for you."

She returned inside while he hesitated, but he couldn't deny her anything. If she wanted to talk, they'd talk—in a manner of speaking.

As he padded through her small living room into the bedroom, he noticed the notebook and pen he'd used the night before already set out on her coffee table. The gesture made his whiskers twitch, though he kept his face turned away so she wouldn't notice.

He shifted as quickly as was safe and dressed in the clothes she'd set out for him—a t-shirt, jeans, and a denim work shirt. Then he went barefoot to join her.

She was in the kitchen, her back to him, working over the stovetop. The scents of bacon, sausage, and eggs made his stomach growl. He snatched up the notebook and started writing as he crossed to her.

"I hope you don't mind the eggs," she said without facing him. "I thought I heard you liked them, but I've got plenty of sausage and bacon if you don't."

He flicked to a clean page to answer her question, then held the notebook up in front of her so she could read it.

"Great. A little of everything then." She started plating food without looking directly at him. "Funny how many tigers don't like eggs."

He pushed the notebook close again, showing her his original note.

She read it and nodded, a slight smile lifting her beautiful mouth. "Yeah, the clothes belong to the Chenikov brothers. They visit occasionally."

His tiger wanted to let out a jealous roar. It was one of the few times Victor really appreciated his mutism—he couldn't inadvertently growl at the mention of the brothers or in any vocal way reveal his possessive challenge. He was perfectly aware that Alexis thought of the three young men as cousins, maybe even siblings, even though they weren't biologically related.

Victor knew Alexis had been watching over the brother since she'd had to take their father in to face the elders for committing one of the worst crimes their kind could commit—killing a human in his tiger form and risking the attention of human authorities. The only thing that had saved Ivan was the fact his mother was an elder. But the crime had had a lot of repercussions for the entire family. On top of it all, the boys took a lot of grief for their father's crime. Alexis had always had a soft spot for them. Just another of her wonderful qualities, he thought, as she continued piling food onto two plates.

"You grab those," she said, nodding to the cutlery as she took the plates to the coffee table. "I usually just eat sitting on the couch. I hope you don't mind. No real need for a table when there's usually just me."

He nodded, following her. They sat on opposite ends. She put as much space between them as was physically possible, but he still felt her. It was like a warm pressure against his skin, and it made eating a lot more difficult than it should have been.

"You felt the others?" she asked, breaking the tension.

He nodded.

"I think they'll wait until nightfall before coming back. There are humans still in the woods, not within my territory but near enough to be at risk. Phoenicia isn't that far away. Nick and the others will wait until they can come at me in their shifted forms."

He agreed with another head bob.

"So, this is a good time to talk, so to speak." She frowned and finally met his gaze. "I'm sorry I'm so awkward. I'm…not sure how to do this."

He raised his brows in question.

"How to have you here while I'm in estrous," she murmured. "How to…resist the instincts."

That he understood. Again, his inability to talk worked in his favor. He didn't have to reveal his own difficulties with this situation. At least not verbally. He had no doubt she could smell his desire, but he couldn't make matters worse with a slip of the tongue.

"So, what we need to discuss…" She shoveled in a mouthful of food and frowned. Finally, she sighed and looked up from the spot on the couch she'd been studying. "Will you get into trouble with the elders for being here? I know if I have to kill one of the others, it'll go bad for me, but if you do…?"

He half-smiled, set his plate aside and wrote his answer. *Since I'm the only one who knows the full security systems at their U.S. and Russian compounds, I should survive.*

She snorted softly.

Beyond that, if I have to kill it will be because they broke the rules of the Mate Run. I won't get into trouble.

She didn't look convinced.

Elizaveta knows I'm here. She supported my decision. She'll make sure whatever happens here doesn't ruin me… more than I'm already ruined.

He grinned as he showed her the note, meaning the last line as a kind of joke, but she didn't smile back.

Okay. Bad joke.

She met his gaze, her expression soft and curious. "We've never spent enough time together to talk about why you don't… can't talk. I know the stories. Are they true?"

Depends on the story.

CHAPTER FOUR

The attack?" she asked, her voice soft.

Victor sighed. *True,* he mouthed.

He'd made a mistake. At four years old, he'd been a silly, adventurous cub with no sense of danger. He managed to get away from his mother's watchful eye while they were on a trip in Montana. He raced into the forest, shifted to his tiger without paying attention to who or what was around, then went for a run. That childish escapade led him into the hands of some very mean men—evil men with knives and guns who had a lot of hatred for a child who shifted from human to tiger.

"Your mother saved you?"

He nodded. His mother had nearly died saving him.

She was shot and stabbed repeatedly yet still managed to tear the three men to pieces and get me to a doctor, he wrote. If not for his mother, he would have died. *She still limps.*

And because she killed humans in tiger form, even though they weren't men who were missed, she ended up in confinement for five years—the extenuating circumstances and the fact she was female meant the elders could avoid inflicting the ultimate punishment of death.

Alexis shifted against the couch cushions, her robe parting across her legs. The flash of pale skin snagged his attention, turning his mind to other, more pleasant thoughts and away from the guilt he always felt when he thought of his mother. He frowned when she pulled the robe closed and kept them on topic.

"I've heard the doctor was able to repair all the damage to your throat. You breathe and eat just fine."

He nodded.

"Then it is a choice? A psychological issue?"

He shook his head. Then wrote, *I physically can't talk. The surgeon operated while I was tiger. He thought I would be okay. But I was young and scared. I rushed the shift back to human. And from that moment on, I couldn't speak.*

"Did they try more surgeries? What did your mother say?"

One more surgery, while I was human. But my mother was afraid to inflict too much more trauma on me at such a young age. Doctor agreed. He attempted to fix the vocal cords, but they were no longer normal. He'd never seen it before and didn't know what to do. We assume the shift after the surgery made some damage permanent.

When she looked up from his note, he shrugged. He knew a lot of the tigers thought he didn't speak because he chose not to—that he had elective mutism. They viewed this as a psychological defect marking him as weak, damaged. He didn't bother trying to change their minds. He knew it was a futile battle.

"Can you make any noise at all?"

A weak, wheezy huff. Very faint. Not the kind of thing I'd want other tigers to hear.

"Ah. Okay."

He smiled, knowing she'd understand. *Sometimes, it's stronger to be silent.*

"And scarier. Your silence is very intimidating."

To the ones who don't think I'm weak for falling prey to a psychological defect?

"No. No one knows what you're thinking. I think all of them are intimidated. They can only judge your mood and thoughts by your scent. Otherwise, they don't know what you might do."

He'd gone to a lot of effort to cultivate that reputation so he wasn't about to argue against it. The tiger world could be cutthroat and dangerous, despite their laws meant to keep things civilized. Any signs of weakness made life difficult. So, damaged as he was, he ensured the others knew he wasn't actually weak.

"Were the years in confinement with your mother difficult?"

She asked so quietly, he might not have heard her if his hearing wasn't so acute.

He'd had to spend the years of his mother's confinement with her as he'd had no one else to look after him. Especially with all the physical help he needed while he healed. His father had abandoned them when she'd given birth to a boy, and that side of the family never claimed Victor. His mother was the last of her line. It was just the two of them, but confinement hadn't been the worst part of his childhood.

Easier than after. We had each other. I got to study, read a lot. We had time to run and even play. Things got harder when she was released. Trying to live among our people again was unpleasant.

She nodded. "The Chernikov boys went through that…are going through it."

He had a great deal of empathy for the boys at that moment. Tigers were never gentle with those they thought vulnerable. He'd re-entered the wider world of their community just as he turned ten and had to do a lot of fighting before the other young males finally left him alone.

Even now, a few occasionally tried challenging him, but his position as head security technician for the elders deflected a lot of the overt aggression. That and the fact he was a vicious bastard in a fight.

Alexis glanced down at her empty plate. "Oh. Guess I was hungry."

The run.

"Thanks for that, by the way. I needed to work out the kinks."

The others might think it was a different kind of run.

"I don't give a damn," she said, and launched off the couch, taking her plate into the kitchen. She faced him from over the island, her hands pressed against the countertop. "Makes me edgy, having all those males just beyond the border of my space. Females don't run in their own territory."

She pushed off from the counter and grunted in irritation. "They've got me cornered. Cornered makes me want to fight."

He jotted a note then crossed to show her. *We could leave. Go somewhere you'll feel less under siege.*

She raised her brows and nodded. "Hadn't thought about that. This is supposed to be my safe place, the place I hunker down and ride things out without worrying about the others intruding." She started pacing the length of the living room.

He leaned against the kitchen island, watching and waiting for her to work through her thoughts. He loved that she thought out loud with him so he didn't have to ask. He loved even more watching her move, all that contained grace and strength like a live wire sparking in the confines of the cabin. Her robe swung around her legs, giving his imagination a lot of delicious ideas, most starting at her ankle and working up the inside of her thigh, and farther.

"Where could we go?" she asked.

Her question brought him back to the present, forcing him to blink away the lovely fantasy he'd been constructing.

"They'll follow," she continued. "But maybe if we stay on the road? We could go into a city…" She shook her head. "No. Not the way I'm feeling. Too twitchy. Don't want to make a scene. Hmm."

She stopped and faced him, her shoulders slumping. "It doesn't matter what I do, though, does it? Even if I get through this estrous without killing someone, there's still the next. And the next." She punched the air and started walking again.

"Fuck. Until I get pregnant, they'll keep coming. To get pregnant, I need to fuck…someone. And when I get pregnant, I'll have to stop being a Tracker. That was always the deal, you know. Once I start having children, I won't be sent out anymore. I can train other Trackers, the way my uncle trained me. But I can't *be* one anymore."

She paused again, and this time when she faced him, a surprising tear dripped down her cheek. The sight of that moisture sent panic shooting through Victor's body. Alexis didn't cry. She couldn't cry. He'd never survive if she cried.

"I've been fired." She sniffled and swiped away the tear with an irritated jerk. "Without even asking if I was ready to start a family. Without telling me to my face that my services were no longer required. *Bastards*."

Flopping onto the couch, she sucked in a deep breath and let it back out with a groan. Her lost expression hurt his soul. Alexis never looked so defeated. She was too strong, too sure of herself. His heart ached seeing her like this, a physical pain that pushed him to ease her sorrow in whatever way he could.

"Now what, Victor? What the hell do I do now? I've been a Tracker since I was nineteen. It's all I ever wanted to do after…"

He saw her hard swallow from across the room. Her pain drew him, an echo of his own, and he couldn't stay away from her any longer.

He sat next to her and pulled her close, hugging her tight. Having her in his arms was torturous, yet also settling. She felt right, the way he'd always imagined. They fit.

Her breath came in a shaking gasp, but to his relief she didn't actually cry.

She pressed her hand against his chest and looked up. For a moment, he lost his balance in the deep blue depths of her eyes. He could live here, in this place and time, for the rest of his life, and die happy.

"Thanks. I'm sorry. This is a little more than I was expecting to deal with. I haven't made a plan for life after being a Tracker." She smiled, though it wobbled at the edges. "Guess I'd better start, huh?"

He nodded and she laughed. The sound made him smile. When he was sure she wasn't going to fall apart, he picked up his notebook again.

Do you want to stay or go? Going will give you time to plan.

"But going is running. The kind of running I don't do." She straightened. "Let them come at me here. If they get killed, it's their own damned fault." Jutting out her chin, she said, "I'd just be defending my territory."

We can make that argument.

She snorted. "We, huh?"

I'm here to help. As long as you need me.

"And there's the next problem," she murmured.

He frowned in question.

"Two more days of estrous. And the only man I want is sitting next to me on my couch."

CHAPTER FIVE

Alexis watched him watching her, waiting for her to say or do more. He held perfectly still, and she knew he wouldn't push her. He wouldn't expect anything she wasn't willing to give.

For him, she was willing to give a lot, though. Only to him.

And, yet, if they went to bed and she got pregnant, would they be allowed to mate? She wouldn't have run. He wasn't allowed to run. More broken laws.

What if she did run? She could simply go long enough for Victor to catch her… No. Still the problem of him being forbidden. The answer wouldn't be that simple.

Hell, she wasn't even sure she was ready to have children, yet the only way out of the Run for her now was to be pregnant and mated. She'd avoided thoughts of family and a future. As a Tracker, death was always an option. She'd had to go after more than one insane tiger in the past. Insane meant unpredictable. Unpredictable could mean death.

She hadn't considered a family because she'd honestly never thought she'd have one. Now she had to consider it. Seriously. She thought of the Chernikovs, of the youngest boy, Mitch, only six months old when his mother committed suicide. Alexis had been sent for his father a few months later, but her every protective instinct had kicked in when she'd seen the boys. She'd taken them in, adopted them—if unofficially—and helped raise them. She loved them deeply.

How much more would she love children of her own?

The idea of her own baby actually grabbed her by the heart and squeezed. Tight.

Huh. Who knew? She did want children. She wanted the family she'd never let herself imagine. She wasn't sure she was ready for it, but she did want it and that was something.

But if she were to have children, she wanted them with Victor. She couldn't imagine creating a family with anyone else.

The realization buzzed through her like an electric shock.

It couldn't work.

She didn't care.

It would work because it was the only option.

"Fuck the elders," she murmured. Then leaned close and kissed him.

Victor remained motionless for several long, torturous moments. She smelled his lust mixing with the scent of hers. The combination made her head spin. The need she'd tried to keep at bay took over. She pushed him back on the couch and crawled on top of him, pressing her body hard against his as she coaxed his mouth open with her lips.

The moment their tongues touched, Victor's resistance crumbled. His arms came around her, crushing her against him. Alexis moaned in pleasure. Yes, yes, yes. Him. Always Victor. Only Victor.

She shoved the denim shirt off his shoulders, then ripped his white t-shirt down the middle, pushing the material apart so she could get her hands on his skin. Everything in her tightened like a spring waiting to launch. She scraped her nails over his chest, leaving light red lines. He arched against her and his hands tightened on her shoulders.

She heard the material of her robe rip and smiled against his mouth. "I guess turnabout is fair play," she said, "but you owe me a new robe." Then she kissed him again.

She moved enough so he could pull off the remains of his shirt without having to stop kissing her. Then she wiggled the tattered scraps of her robe off and settled her naked breasts against his chest. The sizzle of skin on skin contact made her clench and melt at once. More, more, more!

His rough chest hair made her nipples harden into tight, needy beads. She fumbled at his jeans, popping open buttons while still trying not to lose the electric skin contact. He didn't help, much to her frustration. Instead, he stroked her back and shoulders, her sides, then cupped her face. Her every nerve was alive and jumping. His touch soothed and excited, hurt and pleasured at once.

He lowered his mouth to nuzzle her neck. An involuntary groan rose from deep in her chest. She arched against him, pressing hard, clenching her thighs against his hips to ease the tension. It didn't help. Not when his lips were driving her insane.

"Victor." His name came out in a gasp as he edged lower, pushing her up until her small breasts dangled above him. He pulled a nipple into his mouth, sucking hard, scraping her sensitive skin with his sharp teeth. She threw her head back and gripped the cushions. Everything felt so much more intense, sharper, intoxicating. He was exactly what she'd always wanted in a man. Having his mouth on her moved her beyond logical thought. She knew she had to have him.

He moved from nipple to nipple until her body was vibrating with tension. Then, to her surprise, he sat up, taking her with him. A moment later they were in her bedroom. God, his strength… She didn't feel delicate often. Fragility didn't exactly go with her job. But with Victor, she felt safe. She could savor giving up control, letting him overwhelm her and take over.

The feel of his jeans rubbing against her flesh was intolerable. She couldn't stand having any material between them. When he set her on the bed, she wasted no time stripping off the last of his clothing, tugging and ripping until she got to delicious, hot skin. The scent of him filled her, earthy and primal and overwhelming, calling to her inner animal.

She slid down his body, slipping the thick length of his cock between her lips and sucking slowly. She stroked her hands over his hips and thighs, up the flat muscles of his stomach, and indulged herself with the taste of him, that heady mix of salt, musk, and his unique tiger essence that was impossible to describe with human words.

Victor clamped his hands into her hair, hard, almost painful. The pain was a welcome pleasure. When she looked up at him, sun filtered through her closed curtains, casting a pale purple light over him, giving her a sense of moving outside of time. Like the world beyond the room didn't exist. They were suspended in this small bit of time and space, and she had him at her mercy, to do with as she pleased.

His grip tightened further when she slid her lips down his cock. His silence was strange and perfect. Without the distraction of grunts and groans, she was completely focused on her other senses—the taste of his skin, his sweaty heat and bunching muscles, the jolts and jerks of his body when she did something he liked. And his scent... That flavor of spice and musk overwhelmed her, filling her with him, his lust and more.

Their unique essences mixed together, heavy and heady in the small room. Basil and cinnamon and allspice combined with those elements with no names. Somehow it all worked, all fit exactly right. And the result rivaled the most delicious meals, the most luxurious perfumes, the deep heady richness of the forest. It was perfect.

As if they were designed to mingle and become one.

She was so focused on that luxurious, textured scent she almost missed his hands tugging hard at her head. She lifted her mouth from him and raised her brows. He was panting, his beautiful eyes narrowed. She grinned.

"Want me to stop?"

He shook his head, but continued to tug her up the mattress.

"Do I need to stop?"

A nod. Then his mouth was on hers and she gave in to his lead, letting him flip her onto her back while he explored her body in turn with hands and mouth. She closed her eyes, one less sense to rely on, and focused completely on feel and smell, and the taste of him still in her mouth.

Unlike Victor, though, she couldn't keep silent. She moaned when his mouth traveled down the line of her stomach, gasped softly when he licked the skin between her hip bone and curls. She hissed and arched off the bed when his mouth covered her heat and his tongue slipped inside. The play of his tongue, the gentle tease of his teeth, sent her careening into an orgasm, her body shuddering as he held her and kept her from pulling away.

"Victor," she sighed. She opened her eyes when she felt his fingers threading through her hair. His eyes were blacker in the purple light, more startling and beautiful even than normal. She couldn't look away. What was he thinking? He didn't smile, but there was a kind of intensity surrounding him, giving the moment a sacred feel.

What she'd thought was love before felt like a girlhood crush compared to the feeling now crashing over her. It sucked her under like riding whitewater rapids, spinning her around, and tossing her wildly into the air. There was no land, no balance, nothing to hold on to except Victor. In those quiet moments, he captured her loyalty and heart forever. She was done. There would never be another man for her. She didn't have to get pregnant to feel certain Victor was her mate.

She covered his hands where they cupped her cheeks, then rose enough to kiss him. He followed her, keeping his mouth fused to hers. She opened to him, her mouth, her body, her heart. He slipped into her heat as easily as he'd wrapped her soul up in him. His rhythm was hard and slow, deep, steady. The slip and sliding friction of his cock inside her was heightened by the hormones washing through her, and her next orgasm built faster than she expected. She bit his shoulder to hold back but it didn't do her any good. She broke apart with a shout, her hips jerking against his.

He kissed and sucked at her neck without breaking his rhythm, which sent another wash of building sensation through her. She clamped her hands onto his bunching ass muscles and slammed her hips up, meeting him stroke for stroke until he threw his head back, his jaw clenched tight, and came. Silently. Beautifully.

She tried watching his orgasm but her own was just there, on the edge of taking her. She ground her hips against his again, his rough hair rasping against her clit, and she tumbled that final step into bliss.

His weight when he settled over her was wonderfully heavy, pressing her deeper into the bed. As she held him, stroking his back, she pulled in their mixed essences again and set her tiger to memorizing the various components. This was a smell she would never forget. It imprinted on her and made her feel calmer and more whole than she'd felt since her parents were murdered.

Victor was her family now. Funny how it happened. So suddenly. So completely.

But fast on that thought, she had to face how vulnerable they both were now. There was no taking this back. And this broke more laws than she wanted to consider.

Chapter Six

Victor rose up on his arms, braced above her, and raised a brow in question.

Alexis smiled a little. "How did you know I had something to say?"

He ran a hand over her shoulder, rubbing it a little, and she realized she must have tensed.

"You're good with body language."

She giggled when he waggled his eyebrows.

"Yes, yes, that was spectacular. Though we have a little problem now."

His shoulders lifted and fell in a sigh, and then he rolled to her side and pulled her snug against him. With a hand gesture, he indicated she should continue.

"If I end up pregnant, I think they'll let us be. We didn't run, but since you're not allowed to anyway, they can't say you technically broke a law."

He gave her a heavy-lidded look, his mouth flat.

"Right. They might argue the point, but if we are pregnant, they'll have to give us some leeway. Every new cub is important, even if they're males."

He frowned down at her and rubbed a hand over her stomach.

She shrugged. "I know. I wasn't ready to be pregnant yet. With you, though, I'd be willing to have children."

He blinked, then leaned close and kissed her, slowly and with a reverence that clenched tight around her heart. She swallowed hard as he lifted away. She cupped his cheek, not sure she could tell him she loved him yet, but at least through her actions she could show him.

Letting out a shaky breath, she refocused on the point of the conversation. "That said, if I don't end up pregnant at the end of this estrous, the elders are likely to order some kind of punishment. For me, I'm not sure. They'll probably just try forcing me to run again. For you, though, they may impose confinement."

For something like this, Alexis was afraid they might impose a long sentence. Maybe even years. To the depths of her soul, she hated that she might be the cause of him facing that experience all over again. Only this time, he wouldn't receive any special treatment, or any leeway.

He kissed the tip of her nose before rolling out of bed. She curled forward so she could watch him leave the room, now freely admiring his naked body. There was no going back and no point in pretending. When he walked back in, she licked her lips. He shook his head but couldn't hide his slight smile, or the fact his cock was hardening again.

The distraction and fog of lust rushed through her blood. They needed to talk, but right now she wanted nothing more than to roll him under her and fuck him until they were exhausted. He distracted her by holding up his notebook and pen.

She sat up and leaned against the wooden headboard, waiting until he showed her the note.

I knew the risks when I came to help you. I'm not worried about confinement. Been there, done that.

She snorted, waving off his nonchalance. "But I am. I don't want you punished because of me." She pursed her lips and picked at the sheet. "And there's no one else I want as a mate. If you're confined, I'll have to spend all of your confinement fending off other males during my estrous. I *will* end up killing someone."

She glanced at the pad when he raised it in front of her.

Then you'd end up in confinement with me. Could be worse.

That made her chuckle. "True. They can't make me run if I'm in jail. Hmm. Something to consider."

He lifted her chin and shook his head. Then wrote more. *No trying to get yourself confined. You're a female. You can't be sure what choice they'll make. You don't want something worse.*

"Worse? Like being forced into the Mate Run?"

Like being forced to mate with a male of their choosing. No run. An arranged marriage.

She shuddered. "Oh, no. I will not stand for that. I'll vanish into the wilderness before I let them do that to me."

I know. So don't risk it. I want to be able to find you when I get out of confinement.

"You know, we could do that, you and I. We could just vanish."

They'd send the Trackers after us.

"I know how the Trackers work. We could avoid them."

What if we do have children? A girl?

She groaned and punched the mattress. If they had a girl, Alexis couldn't in good conscience keep her from her people. Every female was more valuable than money to the tigers. Females meant survival, and she *did* want her people to survive. She just wanted to choose her own mate, and any daughter she had the same right.

"You're not helping," she said with a grunt.

He cupped her cheek, forcing her to look at him, then he kissed her again. He pulled back and wrote another note.

We'll figure something out. First, we have to get through this estrous. Keep the others from forcing your hand. We'll face the elders after.

He was right. They still had most of the next two days to get through, to keep the other males from forcing her to fight.

She let her gaze move down to his semi-erect cock, then reached out and stroked him. They had two more days to indulge, to take advantage of her cycle. Now that they'd crossed the line, she didn't want to waste a minute.

"Did you notice the way our scents came together?" she murmured. She looked up in time to see him nod, but his focus was on her hand, still moving slowly up and down his cock.

"Perfect."

He nodded again. She squeezed him gently and he sucked in a deep breath.

Ah, she loved the way he felt, so hard and hot and at her mercy. The next two days were going to be fun.

She nudged his shoulder and he eased down onto his back. His hands settled on her hips as she straddled him and lowered herself over his erection, taking him inside slowly so she could savor the stretch and friction. He closed his eyes, gritting his teeth until she dropped the final inch, then he pushed out a breath and looked up at her. She smiled.

"Perfect," she repeated and started to move. She rode him in the same steady rhythm he'd used to command her body earlier. Cool air from an open window washed across her skin, bringing with it the woods, rich soil, earthy bark and leaves. She let all those things suffuse her body and mind, filling her with a rightness she'd never known before.

When Victor's fingers found her clit, she gasped and increased her pace, pounding hard, dropping over the cliff of her orgasm just as he joined her. The feel of him pulsing inside her, the sight of his face tight and straining, was like a dream. She memorized it, living in this moment. For now, at least, he was hers and she was his and there was nothing beyond tomorrow.

CHAPTER SEVEN

When night plunged her room into darkness, Alexis finally left her bed. She pulled on a flannel shirt and a pair of sweats and went to stand on the porch, letting the wind carry the smells of the night to her—dry soil, pine, beech and maple, the tempting perfume of a deer sneaking past the edge of her territory, the crisp combination of fish and damp rock from the river, and a faint tiger musk beneath it all. Her land.

Victor came up behind her, resting his hands on her hips. She leaned into him, smiling at his continued nudity. She really didn't want him dressed again until they had to leave and confront the elders.

A confrontation it would be, too. Alexis had spent her spare moments during the day considering how best to deal with them and had come to a simple conclusion. She didn't run, and she wouldn't run from the elders either. In fact, after twelve years of faithful service, they owed her. She'd earned the right to pick her mate outside the conventions of the Mate Run. She would not allow them to treat her this way.

Her life. Her rules. She'd lived this way since her parents were killed, and she wasn't about to change.

They should have known better anyway. What the hell they'd been thinking when they sent Nick and the others here, she couldn't guess. She dropped her head back against Victor's shoulder and frowned up at the star speckled sky.

"You don't suppose they *want* me to kill Nick or one of the others, do you?"

With a hand on her chin, Victor turned her face toward him and frowned.

"I was just thinking. The elders know me. They know what I'm capable of. They've *used* those skills for years now. They must know trying to force my hand would result in a fight. Do you think they want me to kill someone?"

Still frowning, he shook his head and shrugged at the same time.

"If they did, they could have just said." She'd had to kill before. It was always a last resort, but that's what the Trackers were for: to hunt, capture, and kill if and when necessary. Her uncle had drilled the discipline of the post into her from the time she went to live with him. She didn't kill easily, but she did kill. If they wanted someone dead, why not just send her after them? Why this pretense?

"Unless the tiger they want dead hasn't technically broken any laws," she said. "If he hasn't earned a death-sentence,

I wouldn't go after him. Neither would any of the other Trackers."

She stared into the trees. She could sense the others, just barely, but there at the very edge of her territory, between the distant highway and single dirt road winding through this part of the mountains. They'd crept in closer when the sun set but hadn't started an all out approach on her cabin yet. Could they smell the change from that distance? As soon as they got close enough, they'd know she'd been with Victor. Would it make things worse or better?

Victor took her hand and led her back inside. He gestured to the couch, then went into the kitchen and made them both cups of tea. She loved tea so she was grinning when he handed her the mug.

"Good choice."

He smiled, set his mug on the coffee table and disappeared into the bedroom, returning with his notebook.

Why do you think they'd want one of them dead?

"Why else send them here, without giving me any other advance notice, knowing how angry I'd be?"

Have you considered one of the elders might want you dead?

No. The thought never occurred to her. She was a breeding-aged female and much too valuable to have killed. Allowing her to work the dangerous job of a Tracker had pushed their tolerance. They'd insisted she be trained more thoroughly than any other Tracker. She was the best now, because of their caution.

Maybe that was the problem. Did they worry they couldn't control her? Had she become a liability without realizing it? Was she more dangerous than she was valuable as a female? Given the state of their species, she found it very hard to believe. They needed every single female to mate.

She groaned. She'd just talked herself around to exactly the thing the elders were trying to make her do. They *needed* her to reproduce. So it didn't make sense that any of them arranged for her death.

"If Elizaveta thought any of the other elders wanted me dead, she would have raised more of a fuss."

Victor shrugged in agreement. *Maybe it's exactly as it seems.* He screwed his mouth up into a half-frown, hesitating, then nodded to himself and wrote. *Why were you allowed to become a Tracker? Why did you want to be one?*

Ah. That. "You know my parents were killed?"

An accident.

"No. They were murdered. It was kept very quiet. Another tiger, who loved my mother and was jealous of her relationship with my father, cut the brakes on their car. They never had a chance."

He risked killing you!

His hand actually trembled when he thrust the note at her, and rage filled his normally controlled expression.

She gripped his fingers with one hand and shook her head. "He arranged the 'accident' when he knew I wouldn't be with them. He wasn't crazy. Just jealous."

She let go of his hand and sipped her tea, trying to calm the sudden jump of her pulse. A hard knot of anxiety squeezed her stomach. She didn't talk about this. Ever. Not since she was a child. But she wanted Victor to know the truth.

"My uncle, my mother's brother, was a Tracker. He asked permission to go after the murderer and was allowed to do so by a majority vote. Ten elders to two. Elizaveta took me in while he hunted, in case he didn't come back. Under our laws, she adopted me so I would be protected. I'm still technically her daughter, though she treats me more like a granddaughter."

Victor smiled and took a gulp of his tea.

"My uncle caught the murderer, brought him back to the elders, and was given permission to execute him. Then he retired to raise me. He was my only living blood relative. My father lost his two brothers before I was born—poachers in Russia. My mother only had the one brother. I didn't have grandparents. It was just the two of us."

He trained you?

"Yup."

How old were you?

"When my parents died? Ten. I was fourteen when he finally agreed to start my training. I begged him. I wanted to be the kind of tiger he was, the kind who could protect the ones I loved and take revenge when I couldn't keep my loved ones safe."

Elizaveta allowed it?

Alexis chuckled. "She encouraged it. I'm still not sure why. She fought with the other elders to allow me to work as a Tracker." She stared down into her mug. "Took her a few years. In the meantime, I trained. I had to demonstrate my skills before they'd allow me to take the oath."

Victor edged his notebook into her peripheral vision. She glanced at his question.

Demonstrate how?

"They had me fight," she said. "Four of the other Trackers, none of whom were on my side, which ensured they didn't take it easy on me."

What happened?

"I'm a Tracker now, aren't I? I won."

He raised his brows, and she rolled her eyes.

"Okay, I beat them badly. Four males in their prime, and I sent them packing." Her grin of pride should have embarrassed her, but this was Victor and he'd know she was proud of her skills even if she tried not to show it. "The dissenting elders didn't have much of an argument afterward. I was allowed to take the oath."

You were only nineteen.

She nodded. Her age was part of the legend that grew up around her. Most didn't pass their training to take the oath until their early twenties. But then, most of the other Trackers had less reason to go into the job than she did.

She swallowed the last of her tea and set the mug aside. "As it turned out, my first job was to bring Elizaveta's son before the elders. Ivan…"

She shook her head and stood. When Ivan lost his mate, he went insane. The old story still broke her heart. His three young sons, after just losing their mother to a suicide, then had to lose their father for eight years to confinement. If Ivan hadn't been Elizaveta's, if he weren't so obviously driven mad by his mate's death, he would have been executed. After twelve years, it was still the hardest job she'd ever done. Because she understood Ivan's pain, and her heart ached for his boys.

Needing something to do with her hands, she went back to the kitchen and set the kettle to boil again. She wasn't thirsty anymore, but a second cup of tea felt necessary. She looked back at Victor. "You want another?"

He shook his head.

She occupied herself with putting a fresh tea bag into her mug. Finally, she had to speak into the silence. "So, that's my story. A lot of death and heartbreak got me here."

He rose and stalked to her, his gaze steady. When he took her in his arms, she felt comforted, and comfortable, but not pitied. It made her love him more. She couldn't take him feeling sorry for her. Especially given what he'd been through. She didn't want his pity. She'd become what she was because of her history. While she'd have rather grown up with her parents around, she didn't regret the life she'd lived since or the person she was now. There was no need for anyone to feel sorry for her.

She did want him to know the truth of her past, to understand, and because he was Victor, he did.

Once she'd finished making her next cup of tea, she said, "Let's sit on the porch. It's a nice night. Might as well wait for them in the open."

The other males were circling closer, moving in very slowly. They'd make their way here before the night was out. She wasn't going to cower inside waiting for them.

Victor disappeared into the bedroom long enough to put on some jeans, then joined her on the porch, sitting next to her in one of the two wooden rocking chairs. She contemplated just how sexy he looked in jeans and no shirt. Despite all the time they'd spent in bed, she wanted him again. Heat coiled in her stomach, her muscles tightening with delicious tingles. His scent drifted around her, mingling with her own essence, the perfect combination humming through her body.

She rolled her head, loosening her neck muscles, and focused on the woods instead of Victor. He'd know exactly what she was thinking, but at the moment, they couldn't give in to the chemistry between them. She had to keep her hands to herself. Continuing to stare at him would only make it harder to do.

Chapter Eight

The night wore on with no movement from the other males. Sometime after the clock inside announced it was one a.m., Alexis got up the nerve to broach a topic she was incredibly curious about.

"May I ask you something?"

Victor rolled his head against the back of his chair and raised his brows.

"It's just…given your past, what those human men did to you…do you hate humans?"

He shook his head, his mouth soft and relaxed.

"How can you not? How do you keep from being bitter? I still hate the man who killed my parents, and he's been dead for years."

Do you hate all tigers because of what that one did?

"Of course not. But…the viciousness of the attack on you and your mother, how do you let that go without hating? Or do you still hate those men?"

He stared into the woods for a long moment before he finally started writing.

I don't hate all humans. Those three men were evil. Evil exists—in humans and in tigers—so I can't blame an entire species for the wickedness of some. I'm not bitter because I have no reason to be. I'm alive. My mother's alive. I have a great job, a few good friends. And I spent the day in bed with a spectacular woman. My life is good.

She twisted her mouth in a half-smile, half-grimace at the "spectacular woman" part. "Was it so easy to let go?"

He shook his head. *I was bitter for a while but I grew up. I realized I had too many good things in my life to let the hate fester. The only one it hurt was me. Those men did enough damage. I couldn't let them do any more.*

"That is entirely too healthy," she said. He smiled wide and his shoulders shook with a silent laugh.

She enjoyed the sight of his pleasure, then asked, "How do you feel about Elizaveta's research? You don't hate humans, but could you mate with one?"

Tigers could only reproduce with other tigers. That was one of their biggest problems. Or so it was widely believed. There was a legend among them of a couple in antiquity—a human woman and a male tiger—who not only managed to reproduce but had many children both tiger and human. Most of her people believed the myth was just that, an old romance tale with no basis in fact. The population crisis they were now facing had driven some to consider maybe the myth had a grain of truth. Maybe their salvation was in finding humans capable of breeding with tigers.

The feelings on this topic were strong on both sides—vicious supporters and equally vicious opponents. Some of those opponents thought it was an abomination to even consider reproducing with humans. Others simply thought it would dilute their species and leave them even weaker than they were now.

Elizaveta thought their only long-term hope was to find the genetic descendants of that ancient couple. She was spending a considerable amount of her fortune on genetic and genealogical research.

Alexis wasn't entirely sure where she herself stood on the subject, and she hadn't had her life irreparably damaged by humans. How would Victor feel about it?

I think we can't afford to discount anything that might help us survive. I worry Elizaveta is tilting at windmills though, and even if she's right, there will be a lot of conflict over any tiger/human pairing.

He pulled back the notepad and wrote more, so she remained silent so he could finish what he had to say.

And no, I wouldn't mate with a human. Because you're the only one I've ever wanted.

Alexis sucked in a deep breath. She blinked rapidly. That wasn't the answer she'd been expecting, but it filled her with so much emotion she didn't know what to name any of it.

"Fuck 'em," she said.

Victor straightened and his eyes widened.

She flailed out a hand in a vague gesture. "I don't know what the elders meant by sending the others here. I don't care. I've been a loyal Tracker for twelve years. The only thing I've ever asked was to be released from the Mate Run. They broke their word. If they can't keep their promise with me, I no longer need to be faithful to them."

Victor's brows rose higher and he made a "continue" gesture with a wave of his hand.

"I'm picking my own damned mate outside the Mate Run. They can bite me if they don't like it."

One side of his mouth quirked but he continued staring at her.

She rolled her eyes and looked out into the woods again. "Yes, you're the mate I'm picking. In case you were wondering."

From the corner of her eye, she saw his slight smile and then he faced the trees again, too.

"Don't get smug."

He raised his hands, palms up in surrender.

"And don't pretend you weren't feeling smug." She gave him a narrow-eyed look.

He continued staring into the trees, the very slight upward tilt of his mouth giving him a very satisfied look. She had more to tell him, to admit, and she wanted to try signing it. A tremor of anxiety clenched her stomach. Taking this step felt like laying her soul open for him to see, though she wasn't sure why she was so insecure about it. She'd just told him she intended to keep him. Admitting she'd learned sign language for him shouldn't be any scarier.

She sucked in a breath. She was no coward. He was her mate now. She could do this.

She nudged his arm, and when he faced her fully, she started signing, very slowly. *"The thing is…I've had a thing for you since I was sixteen."*

He tilted his head to one side and frowned, blinking repeatedly as if he wasn't sure he believed what he was seeing.

"Did I sign wrong and say something ridiculous?" she asked aloud. She was pretty sure she hadn't but signing at herself in the mirror was very different from signing to Victor.

He shook his head but didn't otherwise react.

She nodded and went back to signing. *"It was a girlhood crush at sixteen. When I turned twenty, I knew you were the only one I could ever mate with."* She paused and picked at a loose splinter on her armrest, then looked up and finished. *"You're the only one I've ever wanted, Victor. I never allowed myself to hope for this, but now that they've pushed me, I intend to keep you."*

She flexed her fingers, the signing making them ache a little because she really didn't do this enough. Then aloud, because she didn't know all the right signs, she said, "There's not a damned thing the bastards can do about it either."

A few silent minutes passed as he stared, his notebook flittering in the soft breeze. She held his gaze, though it took an act of will to keep from looking away.

Finally, he set the notebook aside and started signing. Alexis tried following but it was clear after a few gestures, real life signing wasn't the same as watching a teaching video. She raised a hand to stop him.

"Sorry," she said, "you're going too fast for me. I've never signed with anyone else before. I can't keep up."

"You can use sign language?"

Her cheeks heated, but she signed, *"I started learning a few years ago."*

"Why?"

"For you."

His mouth actually dropped open slightly, a sign she wasn't sure how to interpret. She couldn't read anything in his expression except the surprise.

"Should I have asked before using sign language with you? Have I offended you or…anything?"

He shook his head, then he met and held her gaze and signed, slowly, *"I noticed you when you were seventeen. The day after you turned eighteen I allowed myself to admit I wanted you. One minute after that, I resigned myself to never being able to have you."*

He paused and his gaze narrowed, but his lips lifted in a bewildered smile.

"You've learned sign language for me." His gesture at himself was brusque.

The astonishment in his expression vanished then, replaced by an unsmiling intensity that made her swallow hard. Heat and passion rose, a sharp, heady mixture of scent and sensation that flowed over her, brushing her skin, filling her nose. She sucked in a deep breath to savor all the things they were saying to each other without words.

He leaned closer. *"If you're willing to stand up to the elders, I will be at your side. Always."*

Her exhale wobbled, but she didn't hesitate when she said, "I am."

He cupped her cheek, stretched across the two armrests, and kissed her. The gentle contact, so at odds with the passion scenting the air and yet so perfectly right, filled her soul. She wanted to burst with the joy of knowing he would stand with her. Every part of her felt alive, sparking with energy and hope.

She gripped his wrist and eased back to smile. "You're mine now, you know."

He nodded, his gaze direct and serious. He touched her chest, right between her breasts, then tapped his own chest. She smiled.

Raising her head, she opened her senses, pinpointing the other males. They'd edged further away from the cabin, still just inside her territory, but some distance from them.

She stood, pulled her shirt over her head and shimmied out of her sweats. "Run with me."

His gaze traveled over her, and her body tightened and tingled in reaction. Then he frowned and nodded in the direction of the other males, even as he stood and stripped off his jeans.

"We'll run the opposite way," she signed, because it was clear to her now she needed the practice. When she made the

clearing, Victor following step for step, she looked around and grinned. "Chase me."

Still in human form, she took off into the trees.

She didn't hear him follow her for almost a full minute, and she knew it wasn't because he was giving her a head start. She laughed, knowing he'd hear, and made her way over the uneven ground. Even on two feet, she was faster than a human woman would have been. Her soles were thicker than a human's, so she could run on the rough soil barefoot and as surefooted as a tiger. This was her territory. She knew every inch of it. So she was a respectable distance ahead when Victor came after her.

She paused long enough to pick up his path, then veered in a new direction. A thrill of excitement with just the barest edge of anxiety bubbled through her blood. She raced between the trees, leading him up a steep hill, then down toward a slow moving river. She didn't even pause at the water but plunged across to the opposite bank.

As she ran, she listened for his pursuit, calculating his distance when he hit the water. Damn, he was fast. He was catching up a lot quicker than she'd have expected.

She loved that.

With adrenaline pumping through her, she finally understood the lure of the Mate Run, why so many females embraced it. It was exciting and sexy making the man you wanted try to catch you. Especially knowing what fun you'd have when he did.

She didn't make it easy on him. So she was surprised when he caught her before she'd planned. She squealed in enthusiastic horror as he grabbed her up and swung her around to face him. She was giggling and panting and more than ready to fuck him when he kissed her.

Wrapping her legs around his waist, she dove into the kiss, feeling free and happy. And so, so right.

She kissed her way down his neck, sucking and biting until he shivered. He cupped her butt and squeezed, his muscles tense and hard everywhere she pressed. He felt so hot, tasted so delicious, she had to have him inside her. Wiggling to get his cock into position, she eased down onto him, taking him in with an easy slide of perfect pressure. He supported her as she moved, harder, faster, the excitement of the chase leaving her so ready she came within minutes.

A moment after her orgasm settled, Victor spun to brace one hand on a tree while still supporting her with the other. He thrust up twice and then dropped his head back and came, his jaw clenched tight. She savored the sight of him, his eyes closed, sweat dripping down the sides of his face, his dark hair damp and begging for her touch, his muscles straining.

When he leaned his head forward again and opened his eyes, he looked directly at her. He didn't have to speak. She saw the intensity of his feelings. A kind of desperate possessiveness filled her, making her cling all the more tightly to him.

"You're mine," she said again.

He nodded.

"I'm yours."

Another nod.

"From now on. I've got your back."

His mouth tilted in a slow, sexy smile, and his eyes grew heavy-lidded. He caressed her back and kissed her in wordless agreement.

She hugged him, settling her face against his neck so she could absorb his essence, now a permanent part of her own. She was so content, so perfectly happy, she took several moments to realize the other males had moved further into her land.

Her head snapped up. The bastards were past her cabin and on their way toward her and Victor's location.

"Son of a bitch." She relaxed her legs and slid to her feet.

Victor kept his arms around her, though, and raised his head. Then nodded and stepped away so she had room to move. She considered their options.

"Shift. We'll face them tiger to tiger. It is time they left my territory." The last came out in a low growl as she started changing.

Chapter Nine

As tigers, Alexis and Victor ran toward the approaching males, who changed direction to come straight at them. They met in an area of tightly clumped trees and little undergrowth. The smells of dark earth, pine, maple, dried leaves and tiger washed over Alexis, and she let loose a territorial roar. The five intruding males spaced out in a half-circle, each pacing a small back-and-forth pattern as they sized up her and Victor.

In this shape, her senses were heightened, and she pinpointed Nick immediately. He stalked forward and back, not an open attack but tempting her to jump him. She quickly assessed the other four. Dev was growling and chuffing, his movements more jerky than the others, his tail flicking in short, hard swipes. The one Siberian she thought she might know but couldn't quite place was hanging back just a bit. Not obvious, but he wasn't pushing forward the way the others were. The two strangers both stalked with tense grace, issuing occasional growls as they watched her.

She crouched, ready to leap if one came at her, and stared at them all, each in turn. Soft sounds of threat and challenge filled the space between the trees. Only Victor was silent, and his silence was a heavy, dangerous presence beside her.

After several moments of display, Nick finally lunged. She was on him immediately, landing on his back, her teeth in his nape before he could get a swipe at her. She drew blood then jumped away. As he turned to face her, she dove in again, plowing through him so he was flipped off balance and thrown into a tree.

While he was down, she bit his neck again, not enough to kill but once again drawing blood, making the threat clear. Nick roared and swiped out, his sharp claws slicing over her side. She growled in irritation more than pain and danced away from him. Nick was a trained Tracker, no easy mark, but she was still annoyed he'd been able to injure her.

She spun around to lunge back at Nick, but Victor leapt first. He caught Nick and rolled him over and over until they both crashed into another tree. Nick ended up on his back with Victor on top, Victor dragging one clawed forepaw over Nick's muzzle. Nick roared again and lashed out, but Victor had him pinned.

Alexis had no time to enjoy watching Victor fight. She whirled to face three of the other four tigers as they came at her. She flipped, turned and swiped at them, holding them at a distance as she regained her balance. The vaguely familiar Siberian remained out of the fight, waiting. But she couldn't worry about him while she was busy handing out a lesson to the three coming at her.

In tiger form, she fought mostly as a normal tiger would, but she had the logic and planning skills of her Tracker training, and she used unexpected moves to toss the three males around. Unlike Nick, none of these were combat trained, and they had no idea how to fight together. She threw one into a tree where he dropped and lay motionless, the wind knocked out of him. Another she managed to hamstring so he went limping out of the fight.

Dev was more aggressive, more desperate than the others. He just kept coming, no matter how many times she tossed him around or made him bleed. He obviously hadn't learned anything when she'd dislocated his shoulder. She'd underestimated his determination.

He caught her, a second gash along her side and a deep one on her hip. She found herself giving ground under his desperate attack. She didn't want to kill him. She might not want him, and she was very annoyed by his inability to take a hint, but he wasn't a bad man. Killing him would be a waste. His instincts were driving him to more violence than the others, though. If he kept pushing, he'd leave her no choice but to take his life.

She glanced around, trying to find a way of ending this without killing. Victor and Nick were still locked in their fight. From her quick glances, she couldn't pinpoint who was winning. The one tiger who'd remained out of the fight was nowhere to be seen. Damn, one more to worry about. She rolled Dev over her back and into a tree, then swung around to face his next attack—which came faster than she'd hoped.

She looked for the missing tiger again, her attention off of Dev for a split second too long. Her distraction made him bold. He barreled headlong into her, wrapping her up in his forelegs so she couldn't catch him with her claws. She roared and chuffed, wriggling and thrashing to throw him off. The bastard was strong and held on, forcing her onto her back. When he got his teeth on her neck, she mentally hissed every curse she knew.

She relaxed just a little so instinct didn't encourage him to actual rip her throat out, then quickly sifted through her options. She didn't have many, not with his teeth pressing through her thick neck fur, tipping against her skin. If she reacted too aggressively, he could seriously hurt her, even kill her. Damn it. Damn it. How the hell did she end up in this position? Trying not to kill the idiot, she'd opened herself up to getting killed. A mistake she'd never make again.

Slowly, she tried moving her head, but his jaw quivered with tension, warning her to stop. She stilled, fighting her own instinct to thrash. If he thought she was giving in, he'd raise his head and she could throw him off. But seconds ticked past with his mouth still on her, her breathing harsh in her own sensitive ears.

Her patience wore thin, her ability to remain passive never one of her strong suits, and then she felt his jaws start relaxing. She held herself tight and ready for the instant he lifted his mouth from her throat. Before she could act, another tiger drove into Dev's side, flipping them both away from her.

She rolled to her feet, assuming her helper was Victor, until she heard the tiger roar.

Before she fully processed the shock of that sound and the help from the fourth tiger, a silent Victor flew past her and joined the others. He and the vaguely familiar Siberian moved like they'd fought together before. Their attack was coordinated and flawless, beautiful in its way. They drove Dev back, reluctant inch by reluctant inch. The Bengal tried to get past them, to fight back, but he wasn't trained and was no match for the two.

Alexis dragged her attention from the fight to confront the remaining three males. The two she'd beat were slowly slinking away, taking the fastest route out of her territory. Nick remained but he sat off to the side, a casual position conveying an end to his aggression. She kept him in her peripheral vision just in case and turned back to the battle between Victor, the Siberian, and Dev.

The sounds of their fight echoed through the trees, roars that would terrify any humans in the area. She was glad she and Victor had run a circuit of her lands just that morning. No humans were near, and the chances of them getting in over the course of the day without her knowing were low. The last thing they needed was an unfortunate camper reporting sounds of big cats fighting.

Dev was scrappy and hard to put off. Despite being severely out of his depth, he kept attacking, roaring in response to each of the Siberian's vocal challenges. Victor's silence was somehow loud in the noise, too obvious to be ignored. Dev fell back under the two tigers' coordinated moves but refused to leave.

Then Victor rammed into his side, moving as fast as any tiger she'd ever seen. One moment, he and the Siberian were working together, the next, Victor was a silent savage, tearing at Dev's sides and flank. The Bengal's roar turned from aggression to pain, and a moment later, he disappeared into the woods. Unlike the others, he didn't slink away. He tore off toward the closest exit from her territory. Alexis smelled the sharp tang of blood in his wake. Not enough to kill him, but enough to leave him weak for the next few days.

Obviously, Victor didn't feel the same need to pull his punches as she did.

She smiled, her whiskers twitching, her tail flicking with nervous unspent energy.

No one moved until the retreating Dev left her lands. Then everyone converged on the center of the combat area. Victor walked alongside the other Siberian. She joined them, staying closer to Victor than the others. Finally Nick stood and approached, remaining out of single lunge range.

The rest of this situation would require conversation. Shifting where she stood, she let her body flow and stretch, the sounds of popping muscle and bone and the slight aches that always came with the change almost comforting in their familiarity. Her wounds would follow her into her human form, but the shift would help speed up the healing. None of her injuries were bad enough to prevent her from returning to human thankfully, though it hurt more to shift while wounded.

When she finished, she blinked several times to adjust to seeing the world through human eyes and shook, tossing off the residual tingling of the change. Then she looked around. Nick and Victor were just finishing their shifts. The remaining Siberian waited until Victor finished and nodded at him, then he began his change.

Interesting. She studied this male who was obviously well known to Victor. Who was he? She was embarrassed to admit she had no idea who Victor's friends were. How could she feel so close to him and yet know so little about his daily life? An oversight she intended to fix. He was her mate now. She would learn everything there was to know about him.

They waited silently for the Siberian to finish his change, the cool night air whisking away their sweat. She used the time to inspect Victor for injuries. He had a few red lines that were already disappearing. To her satisfaction, Nick had a cut along his chest deep enough it was still leaking blood. No wonder he'd stepped out of the fight with Victor. She gave her own injuries a quick glance. The deep one on her hip was sealed but still a very angry-looking, raised welt. Most of her other cuts were almost healed.

Once the Siberian was in human form, Alexis finally recognized him. He was tall and wide, with dark brown eyes. His dark hair was cut tight to his head. She couldn't remember his name—they'd never actually been introduced—but she'd seen him before at the elders' West Virginia compound. He worked as a security technician on the team Victor headed.

She felt silly for not realizing the two men were more than just colleagues. This was the man she'd once seen use sign language with Victor.

The man smiled at her, and then started signing to Victor who answered in kind. She watched for several moments, trying to keep up, but they were too fast. Obviously they did this often. Yes, she definitely needed to practice with real people. So much for the fluency she'd thought she'd developed.

"I'm Joseph," he introduced himself while still signing with Victor. "Pleasure to finally meet you, Alexis."

She nodded at his hands. "Victor can hear you. Why are you still signing?"

He shrugged. "Habit. I translate for him at work occasionally, during some meetings so he doesn't have to write everything he wants to say." He made a series of rapid gestures to Victor, who glared at whatever Joseph had said. Then aloud, and with a slight smirk, he added, "Elizaveta sends her regards."

"She sent you to help?"

"To make sure no one died."

A growl rose from deep in her chest. The elders *knew* someone might die, enough so that Elizaveta felt the need to send Joseph even after Victor told her he was coming to help, so why the *hell* had they started all this? Irritation made her growl again, and Victor raised his brows. She shook off his silent question. She almost signed "later" but stopped herself, conscious of Nick watching the exchange. She still didn't want anyone but Victor knowing she'd learned sign language. It wasn't anyone else's damned business.

Nick chose that moment to step closer. "Elizaveta is interfering in what the other elders have declared appropriate. Alexis has to run."

"Far as I can tell, she did already," Joseph said, his hands still moving in translation. "And she chose Victor here as her mate for this estrous."

"No. He can't run."

"You'll have to take that up with the elders. None of my concern. Though Elizaveta did make a point of saying nothing in the decree said Victor couldn't mate. He just isn't allowed to run. Nowhere does it say Alexis couldn't pick him while he was standing still."

Joseph signed something to Victor, who answered, but most of Victor's focus was on Nick. Alexis filed Joseph's comment away for later consideration. She hadn't realized there was a loophole in Victor's exclusion from the Mate Run. That Elizaveta knew it and had never mentioned it was something she intended to talk to her adoptive mother about.

She couldn't be too upset with the older woman, though. Alexis hadn't ever come out and admitted she wanted Victor, not to anyone. She'd actually tried to hide her feelings for him, because she knew she wasn't allowed to have him. But she'd deal with that later. Now, she considered Nick.

"Why are you pushing this?" she asked him. "We were colleagues."

"You're special, Alexis. You deserve better than someone who's damaged."

"That's not your call."

"You shouldn't be wasted on a mentally weak tiger." He flicked a glare at Victor. "The elders want you with someone strong."

"I don't see any mentally weak tigers around. And again, it's not the elders' call any more than it's yours."

Victor started signing fast, and Joseph translated.

"We're done here, Nick. You've made your play and lost. Go tell the elders it's finished. She's chosen. If they have a problem with her choice, they can face both of us to explain."

"You're making a mistake, Alexis," Nick said. "It will affect your children. Can you really do that to them? You risk them having a mental disease just to be with him." He jerked his head in Victor's direction without looking at him.

"Time to leave, Nick," she growled, fury lacing her voice. She wasn't going to convince him Victor wasn't defective, but she was so angry at his attitude and willful ignorance, she was a single word away from attacking him again.

He nodded, turned his back to Victor and Joseph as a clear sign he wasn't worried about them, and walked away without changing back to tiger.

Chapter Ten

Alexis waited until she was sure Nick was really leaving, then turned on Joseph in time to see him and Victor exchanging a few more signed words, none of which she caught.

"What were the elders thinking?" she demanded.

Joseph glanced at Victor, then back at her. "I'm not privy to their logic. You'll have to ask them."

Victor signed something which Joseph answered silently. Victor started signing furiously, moving in sharp, choppy bursts.

Joseph held his hands up. "Hey, I'm just here to help. Don't yell at the messenger."

Joseph signed to Victor, and this time Alexis managed to understand the full sentence, *"I'm out of here."*

Aloud, he said, "My job is done. You two have fun." He waved goodbye and wandered back into the woods, heading in the same direction as the others but at a more leisurely pace.

For a long moment, Alexis stared at Victor. The sun was painting the sky pink, layering shadows beneath the trees. They had to get home soon, but she didn't move immediately.

Finally, Victor nodded toward her cabin.

"Wait. Wait. I…" She paused, then signed, *"I'm sorry. I would have prevented all this if I'd known."*

"It's not your fault. Why are you apologizing?"

"I don't know. I feel like I should have expected this…or something." She flexed her fingers and grimaced.

Victor smiled. *"You need more practice so your fingers don't hurt. It takes time."*

"I thought I was pretty good, even though I needed you to go slow, then I watched you and Joseph." She shook her head and snorted a half-laugh. *"I do need more practice."*

"You said you've been learning for years but never signed with anyone else before. Why not?"

She felt her cheeks heat and glanced away as she admitted, "I didn't want anyone to know I was learning. I was afraid the others would figure out I was doing it for you, that they'd see how I felt. I was afraid…" She swallowed hard and made an effort to sign the rest. *"I was afraid one of the males would decide you were a threat and try to kill you. I don't know. Ridiculous, right?"*

"Not ridiculous. All tiger males are jealous of other males and possessive of the females. You lost your parents to a male's jealousy."

She'd never thought of it that way. She just hadn't wanted anyone to know what she was doing. He was right. The way she'd lost her parents had made her more sensitive to how males reacted to others they saw as rivals. She hadn't wanted anyone to see Victor as someone who needed to be eliminated.

"You were afraid for me?"

She nodded.

"Why?"

His question made her blink. "That's a silly thing to ask." She closed with him, leaving just enough space so that she could sign. *"I love you, Victor. I have for years. How do you not know that?"*

Victor stared at her as if she'd just hit him with a tree limb.

"What's wrong?"

He didn't move. His expression was serious, but it was otherwise impossible to judge the emotions in his gaze. A knot tightened in her stomach as the moment stretched. Until he'd come to help her, she really hadn't thought Victor felt anything special for her. Over the last two days, she'd come to believe he returned her feelings. Maybe not love, but he cared for her. He wouldn't have come all this way if he didn't.

Right?

Victor wanted her, but lust wasn't love.

She swallowed around a thick lump in her throat and turned away. "We'd better get back. It'll be too light soon. I'm too tired to shift right now." She wasn't physically tired. She could easily go tiger again. But mentally…mentally she was drained.

She hurried away from him, only half listening for him to follow. Then his hand was on her arm, stopping her. Facing him would hurt. She didn't want to, but he couldn't talk to her unless she did.

Squeezing her eyes shut, she counted to ten, then blew out a breath, opened her eyes and turned.

He cupped her cheek, a gesture that was more painful than any gentle touch should have been, and kissed her—his mouth soft, his lips firm against hers. She allowed the contact but didn't return the kiss.

When he eased back, she rubbed her lips together and waited for him to do something else, but she couldn't quite look at him.

He lifted her chin until she either had to face him or make some extreme contortions to avoid eye contact.

Then he signed, *"I love you, too. Silly woman. Didn't I tell you that already? Since you were eighteen. Why are you suddenly doubting?"*

"You didn't say you loved me. You said you wanted me. Then, just now, you didn't say it back. You looked at me like I'd gone nuts. I don't know." She scowled and jerked her hands up, palms toward the sky. "I've never told anyone I loved them before. I was expecting a different response."

He cupped her chin and mouthed, I love you. Then went back to signing. *"I love you. I want to have a family with you. I never thought I'd be able to, but now I have no intention of letting you go."*

Her smile came slowly, shyly. He did love her. Her heart swelled as she gazed at him. They still had one major obstacle, though. *"We still have to get around the elders."*

He nodded. *"We will."*

Alexis took his face between her palms and kissed him, hard and sure. Her need rose up as she pressed against him, her naked skin sensitive and warm everywhere they touched. His hands on her back left trails of tingling heat. She was wet and ready for him—so quickly, so easily.

With a breathless chuckle, she untangled herself from his arms. "At the cabin," she said. "Too much daylight."

He nodded, gripped her hand, and took off at a run. She squealed in shock, stumbled the first step, then caught her balance and kept pace with him, laughing as they raced home.

Home. He was always welcome in her territory now. The thought filled her with peace.

Chapter Eleven

Victor didn't pause when they reached her front door. He dragged her inside and straight to her bedroom.

She loved him.

The idea was still so overwhelming he had trouble believing he'd actually seen her sign the words.

When he had her in the purple darkness of her bedroom, he pulled her close and kissed her, all the emotion he'd spent years suppressing pouring out.

She loved him.

He intended to show her just how much he loved her, too. Her doubt was still almost as amazing as her love.

He kissed his way across her jaw, down her throat, and reveled in the shivers that shook her when his teeth skimmed lightly along her collarbone. He ignored his insistent cock and laid her on the bed, needing to worship her more than he needed anything else in the world. She sprawled under him, looking at him with her beautiful blue eyes, heavy-lidded and sexy. Her short hair was tousled from the skirmish, her skin flushed, her nipples peaked. He'd never seen anything more erotic.

He leaned down and kissed her, tangling his tongue with hers, tasting and savoring. Then he moved down, across her chin, licking a wet line over the sensitive skin on her neck. The thought of that Bengal having his teeth on her throat earlier sent a roar of rage through his blood. If the male had done her any serious harm, Victor would have ripped him into little shreds. To replace the memory, he took his time gently kissing and licking her throat—to excite her and soothe his own soul. She wasn't hurt. At least not anything permanent.

She was his.

He continued his slow exploration down the very center of her chest, licking his way between her breasts. When he moved lower without taking one into his mouth, Alexis grabbed his hair and tried pulling him up. He resisted with a grin, and once she loosened her hold, he continued downward, keeping his attention focused on the imaginary line. Her stomach quivered under his lips. The sounds of her pants and moans filled the large room. God, he loved those sounds. He had never been more grateful for the gift of his hearing than he was at that moment, as he relished her reactions to him.

At her navel, he paused to torture her a little, licking a wet circle around the indentation, and then blowing cooling air across her skin. She gasped and jerked up. So he did it one more time before moving lower, kissing to the top of her curls before stopping again. The frustration in her groan filled him with satisfaction. Torturing her was the most deliciously fun antidote to the fear he'd experienced during the fight, seeing her fall under the Bengal.

He hovered just above her and took a few moments to examine the remains of her wounds along her waist and hip. She was healing fast, as their kind did. The hip injury had been the worst, but all that remained now was a thick red line. He was grateful she wasn't more badly injured, so grateful she was strong and able to defend herself.

He would be forever in Elizaveta's debt for not stopping him from coming here to help when Alexis needed him. Thanks to her, he had the woman he loved, alive and healthy and his.

The truth of that would probably take weeks to sink in. As he breathed in her cinnamon and allspice scent, and the perfect way it mixed with his, he looked forward to reminding himself again and again that Alexis was really his mate.

The lure of her drugged him and he couldn't resist her any longer. He kissed over her hipbone, then settled between her thighs and licked her heat, teasing her open with his tongue and fingers. She gasped and writhed as he held her in place, making her feel every last lap of his tongue against her most sensitive skin. Then he turned his attention to her clit and steadily pushed her into an orgasm that made her scream. It filled him with a primal sense of rightness.

Before she fully recovered, he slid into her, overwhelmed by the tight heat wrapping around his cock. So fucking *right*.

He would never feel completely whole again without her at his side.

His mate.

He came in a state of mindless bliss, his soul bursting with the love she had for him.

A few moments later, cradling her in his arms, his brain started functioning again as he considered their future. Including the information Joseph had passed on. Something Alexis needed to know.

First, though, he wanted to remind her she could trust him. *"I love you,"* he signed.

She looked into his face and smiled, her expression soft and relaxed. "I love you too. I'd sign it, since I know I need the practice, but I like where my hands are right now."

She had one snuggled against his side and the other drawing gentle circles low on his abdomen. Since he liked her hands where they were, too, he wasn't about to argue.

"You don't mind?"

He shook his head. How could he mind? He loved her touch. *"I'm still amazed you learned. And that you kept it secret all these years. You're doing well for someone who hasn't signed with other people."*

"Thanks. But it's pretty clear I need more practice *with* someone."

"I'm looking forward to helping."

"Me too." She smiled, then pursed her lips. "Can I ask…? You and Joseph. I know you work together, but you're not just colleagues are you?"

"No. Joseph is my oldest friend. Probably my only real friend."

"Besides me," she said, with her bottom lip thrust out in a little pout.

"Now, besides you. But we've only just become friends." He sat up a little higher against the headboard. *"Are you able to follow my signing?"*

"You're going slow enough." She nodded.

"Good. As for Joseph, I've known him since I was ten. He helped me when some of the other young males tried to jump me. We fought them off together and have been friends ever since."

"I'm glad," she murmured as she rose up a little and kissed him. "Everyone needs a friend."

"And you? Who are your friends?"

"Well, the Chernikov brothers. And Elizaveta…"

"They're more like relatives. Do you have a good friend?"

"I'm friendly with some of the Trackers, but I guess I've kept my distance." She shrugged. "I've always kept a distance with the others in case I had to go after them one day."

The admission broke his heart. *"You don't have to keep any distance between us. Not anymore."*

"I love you, too."

He paused to consider what he had to tell her. Finally, he signed, *"How much of what Joseph and I said after the fight did you understand?"*

"You were signing too fast. I only picked up a few words. I understood elders, and my name, maybe a few other words, but not enough to follow the conversation. Why do you want to know?"

"So you didn't understand when he said you had a nice ass?"

She shifted positions so she could sign as well as saying it aloud, "That's very sweet. Tell him I said thank you."

Victor glared.

"What? You expected me to be insulted?"

Her grin made him glare harder. *"I wasn't expecting you to be pleased."*

She laughed. "Which is why I am. What else did he say—besides complimenting my ass?"

He shook off his vague sense of jealousy and said, *"Elizaveta didn't just allow me to help you. She didn't just send Joseph to help us. She…"* He paused, not sure how to tell her.

Finally, he went with the way she'd want to hear it—blunt and without ceremony. *"Elizaveta organized everything. She made sure the other elders decided it was time for you to run. She instigated the discussion leading to them sending Nick and the others here. She planned all of this."*

"Wait," she said, sitting up fully to face him. "Nick said she argued against this. Now you're telling me she made it all happen—me being fired, forced to run…all of this is her doing?"

"She intended for us to mate. Apparently, in her words, she was tired of us mooning around after each other."

"She had me fired without warning and sent all those males here *without warning me*. She gambled on you and I breaking all the rules I've been upholding for the last twelve years. What the fucking hell, Elizaveta?"

She launched out of bed to stalk the length of the room. "She risked me having to kill innocent men who were just doing what they believed they were allowed to do. She risked you being killed in the fight. She risked me being injured because I would rather fight than run. And she did it all on the *chance* we would mate?"

Victor let her rant. He wasn't entirely sure how he felt about Elizaveta's machinations either. He was happy to finally be with Alexis. Stunned to be able to love her freely. Given what could have happened, though, his gratitude to the elder was somewhat tempered.

On the other hand, he wasn't sure how he felt about Alexis' anger. She seemed to be forgetting that because of Elizaveta, they were together. Did she regret being with him now? Did she resent it?

They still had the problem of her future estrous cycles. They couldn't technically be permanently mated until she got pregnant. If they didn't get pregnant today, because of Elizaveta, Alexis would be forced to run again. And to fight again. Tigers didn't get pregnant quickly. He could tell by her scent she wasn't yet. There would be a tell-tale shift in her hard-to-define pheromone fragrance, a sweet, earthy flavor added to her normal essence when she conceived.

So where did all this leave them?

Did she love him enough to keep picking him each cycle, despite what the elder had done to her?

Alexis paused in her tirade to stare out the window at the bright morning. Damn Elizaveta. Damn her for starting all this without so much as warning her! She manipulated and organized and risked other peoples' lives. All for what?

For Alexis to be with the man she loved.

Damn, damn, damn. She couldn't even hate Elizaveta for her interference because now Alexis got to have Victor.

She narrowed her eyes. As far as the other elders were concerned, if Alexis wasn't pregnant by the end of this estrous, she'd need to run again. And again. They'd keep throwing Nick at her in the hopes of her giving up on Victor—who couldn't run but apparently could stand there and be chosen. She snorted at that. Loopholes. Leave it to Elizaveta to find such an absurd and effective loophole.

Loopholes…

If Elizaveta had found a way for Alexis and Victor to mate during one estrous, surely she'd und a loophole allowing them to be together permanently. She had to know Alexis wouldn't put up with any more cycles like this one. Was there some way they could stay together without getting pregnant? Or was she just hoping Alexis would get pregnant and make the matter moot?

Rubbing her hands over her head, then digging her fingers into her hair, she contemplated the options. She came to one conclusion.

"Fuck the lot of them."

She faced Victor so she could see his reaction as she continued. "Let's get married. Tomorrow. Let's go to Vegas and get married."

"Even if you're not pregnant?"

"Elizaveta wanted us to stop 'mooning' over each other, right? She wanted us to end up together. She went to all the trouble of pointing out there was a loophole in the decree that you couldn't run. She can come up with some way for our marriage to be okay. Even if she hasn't already, she can figure something out. She owes us after all this."

She crossed to the bed and sat down next to him, this time signing, *"I love you. Whether we have children or not, you're my mate."* Then aloud, "The elders will just have to deal with it. I'll always fight rather than run. I will always choose you, no matter who they send at me. This thing between us is done. Elizaveta is so good at manipulating everyone; she can continue doing it now."

With a snort, she added, "I bet she already has a plan in place. She knows me too well."

"She would guess you'd propose to me?"

Alexis grinned. "Yes. We'll probably see her in Vegas. Come away with me. Marry me." She kissed him, a brief brush of lips. "If we're lucky enough, have children with me."

Victor took her cheeks in his hands and stared into her eyes, studying her so closely she would have squirmed if this was anyone but him. With him, she could be open, herself. With him, she didn't have to hide. And it made her love him all the more.

He leaned back and signed, *"You're sure? You won't regret this?"*

"Oh, Victor." She signed, *"I love you. I've loved you my entire adult life. I could never regret this, us."* Aloud, "What do you say?"

"I'll get a tux when we get there."

She smiled then laughed. Then kissed him. As they dropped back to the bed, Alexis wrapped herself in his love. They would have children together. They would have a life. She would love him until her last breath. A love she intended to defend with as much determination as she'd defended her peoples' laws. So what if she was breaking laws to have him. That's what meddling elder mentors were for—finding loopholes and ensuring Alexis got her happily ever after. Whether the others liked it or not.

Because Alexis liked it, and Victor, very much.

"I love you," she said against his mouth, and though his hands were too occupied for him to return the sentiment, she felt his love in every move he made. A silent, potent, perfect love.

Read on for an excerpt from

ALONG CAME A TIGER

(Tiger Shifters 2)

CHAPTER ONE

Ridley Creek State Park outside Philadelphia

Daniel Borowski stared through the darkness at the sleek black Jaguar parked in front of an isolated home at the edge of the park. The bastard with Sarah sat sideways, his profile visible through the back window. Daniel had no trouble discerning Bradley Williams' dark blond hair and blue eyes, even in the dark. Tiger-shifter eyesight was handy that way. He only saw the back of Sarah Chu's head, but he knew it was her.

He'd know Sarah anywhere.

His lip curled as he watched the two. Bradley was the kind of slick, rich asshole who always set Daniel's teeth on edge, but this man's pretty boy exterior hid a murdering evil that sent Daniel's instincts into overdrive. Especially when the bastard was sitting next to Sarah.

Daniel dug his fingers into the bark of a fallen tree in front of him, trying to rein in his anger.

"You're sure you don't need help?" Alexis Tarasova asked from beside him.

He kept his gaze on the car, swallowing a growl as Bradley touched Sarah's cheek.

"I'll be fine," he answered in a tight murmur, hoping his mentor wouldn't pick up on the rage he heard in his own voice. Alexis might have been retired for ten years, but she was still one of the best Trackers he'd ever known. He was a better Tracker for her training. Sometimes, though, her perception was inconvenient. Right now, he needed her to concentrate on her part of this situation, not his straining control. "It'll take both of you to keep Joseph away."

He glanced at her, taking in her focused stare. Beside her, her husband Victor Romanov waited so silently Daniel might have forgotten he was there, if he couldn't sense him.

To the west, not far from their position in the trees surrounding the front of the house, Daniel also sensed Joseph Bennett in his tiger form, waiting for his chance at revenge against the man who'd killed his sister. Joseph was so full of rage he wasn't thinking straight.

Neither was Sarah.

Daniel looked back to the car in time to see the bastard lean toward Sarah and say something close to her ear. Daniel snarled.

Alexis nudged his arm. "Victor can handle Joseph if you need me. The point is *not* to kill the human."

"I haven't forgotten why we're here."

"You sure? Because you're stripping bark off that log."

Daniel scowled down at his hand. His fingers were buried in the thick bark. Fuck. If he couldn't calm his temper, he would ruin everything. He was a Tracker. He should be able to control himself.

For Sarah's sake, he *had* to control himself.

"I'll be fine. Just make sure Joseph doesn't get anywhere near that man. You have a place to…hold him until he's thinking straight again?"

Alexis signed something to her husband, who signed back. Daniel didn't understand sign language so he waited for Alexis to finish.

"We'll take him to Victor's retreat near the Canadian border. That should be far enough from Philly to keep him out of trouble."

Alexis narrowed her eyes and her mouth tightened. The reaction was telling.

"You don't think he'll calm down, do you?" Daniel asked, facing the car again.

"Would you if Williams had murdered your sister?"

"No." He'd want to rip out the man's throat and drink his blood. He was already itching to tear him to pieces, and that was just for *touching* Sarah. He could only imagine what Joseph felt.

Or Sarah for that matter. Su-jin had been her best friend. Sarah's rage and need for revenge no doubt matched Joseph's— strong enough for her to risk her own life.

Among their people, killing a human being, especially in tiger form, was an automatic death sentence. There had been a few exceptions over the years, but that was before forensic science had improved so significantly.

There would be no leniency for Joseph, even given the circumstances. Killing a human risked exposing them all to the human world. Their people were already on the brink of extinction and desperately struggling to survive. They couldn't afford for the general human population to learn that tiger shapeshifters existed.

Sarah might not be put to death because she was a rare female tiger, but she would be caged for life if she went through with this. Daniel couldn't allow that. He loved her too much to let her to throw her life away.

"He's getting closer," Daniel said, jerking his head in the direction of Joseph's approach.

A soft growl carried through the dense woods, quiet enough only the tigers would be able to hear it. The enraged tiger knew they were there to stop him and he was warning them off.

Alexis glanced at Victor, then back at Daniel. "Good luck. Keep her safe."

Daniel nodded and watched as she and Victor slipped into the darkness under the trees. As they disappeared, he glimpsed Victor begin to disrobe. He would shift into his tiger shape while Alexis stayed in human form. Between them, they'd be able to handle Joseph, no matter how angry the man was. At least Daniel hoped so. As a former Tracker, Alexis had handled worse. But Joseph was Victor's best friend. They'd try not to hurt him.

Daniel focused on the car again. Joseph was their responsibility. He had to trust Alexis and Victor to do their part.

His job right now was to get Sarah out of this, unharmed. And to avoid killing the bastard with her.

He pulled in a deep breath, letting the warm, humid summer air clear his head. The scent of beech, oak, fresh cut grass, and soil settled him. He waited and listened to the others as they closed with Joseph. Then he rose from his hiding spot beside the drive and approached the car on Sarah's side. The gravel covered driveway barely crunched under his light footsteps.

He snatched open Sarah's door before Williams realized Daniel was there. Sarah, on the other hand, glared up at him. He knew she'd felt him approach. Hell, she'd known he was in the trees.

For a split second, the dark power of her gaze stilled him. Even angry, she was the most beautiful woman he'd ever known. Black straight hair hung over her shoulders. The car's interior light threw shadows across her sharp features, highlighting high cheekbones and the beautiful tilt of her dark brown eyes. Without thought, his gaze dropped to her mouth—those full lips had always captivated him. Right now, they were pressed tight together, and her jaw was clenched.

He blinked and forced himself to remember why he was here.

"Out," he ordered. "Now. We're leaving."

"Who the hell are you?" Williams demanded.

"Her fiancé," Daniel easily lied. As far as he was concerned, it was only a partial lie anyway.

"You shouldn't be here," Sarah hissed.

This close, the smell of Bradley Williams' lust and strangeness punched at Daniel. Though it was a subtle texture, impossible for Daniel to describe in human words, he could tell from Williams' scent the man wasn't sane, and his lust wasn't for sex.

Despite Daniel's best effort to control his temper, he snarled, a low animal sound rising in his throat. He swallowed down the instinctive challenge and reached a hand out to Sarah.

She ignored it. "It's none of your business what I do," she said.

"This *is* my business."

"You heard the lady," Williams said. "She wants to be here. Looks like your engagement is off. Beat it."

Daniel kept his gaze on Sarah so his tiger didn't get the best of him. He quickly unfastened her seatbelt and pulled her from the car. "I understand why," he whispered into her ear. "Believe me. I understand, but it will only hurt you. I will not allow that."

She jerked free of his hold as soon as her feet were under her. "What I do is not up to you, Daniel."

Williams jumped from the car, slamming his door shut behind him. "What the hell do you think you're doing? Do you have any idea who I am? I will have you thrown in jail for this."

The irony of that comment almost made Daniel laugh. He finally looked the other man in the face, letting him see his anger, and his animal.

Williams stopped short. Some small part of him was sane enough to recognize death when he faced it. Unfortunately, he wasn't sane enough or afraid enough to let that knowledge stop him for long.

"The lady wants to be with me," Williams said with a smirk. "If you don't get the fuck out of here, I'll make sure you're ruined."

"I'll leave right now. With Sarah." He looked down at her. She was a foot shorter than his 6'3", but her stature belied her stubborn will. He scented her anger, a complex acrid punch overlaying her natural scent, and he knew she'd fight him. He couldn't blame her wanting to kill Williams, but throwing away her life for revenge wasn't an option.

"Daniel…" she warned, the quiet edge of tiger in her voice.

He put his face close to hers, their noses almost touching. "I'm not leaving without you."

When she didn't respond, he gripped her arm and started toward the trees, and the path that would take them off Williams' property back to the side road where Daniel had parked his truck. She jerked her arm, trying to pull free, but he refused to let go.

Suddenly, Williams was in front of them, grabbing Daniel's arm in a solid, strong grip and stopping him and Sarah in their tracks. The man's strength and quickness were impressive for a human. Surprisingly so.

Despite Williams' best efforts, though, Daniel refused to drop his hold on Sarah. Whatever strength the man's psychosis gave him, he wasn't strong enough to beat an angry male tiger in a contest of wills.

"Let her go, asshole. Or I swear…"

"What?" Daniel asked, his voice low.

"You won't want to live when I get done with you."

Daniel stared into Williams' eyes and saw just how crazy he was. A deep, dark insanity robbed him of any humane qualities. If Daniel had been a human man, maybe even a less well-trained tiger, he might have been scared. After all, this man had succeeded in capturing, torturing, and killing one of their people—no mere human woman, but a tiger with speed, strength, and rapid healing far outstripping any human.

Granted, Su-jin wasn't as strong as most tigers, but even the weakest of their people could overpower a single human. Most of the time. That this man had held her against her will meant he wasn't to be taken lightly.

A growl lodged in Daniel's throat. He forced down the need to meet Williams' challenge, though every instinct screamed at him to attack and kill the human. Especially because Williams was a threat to Sarah. Daniel couldn't afford to answer the threat. The point of being here was to get Sarah away without either of them killing the human.

He held the man's stare without responding and waited for him to let go.

In the distance, Daniel heard the sounds of a tiger fight— at least one side of it. Victor was mute in both human and tiger form, so there was only the sound of Joseph's chuffs and growls.

Williams' eyes narrowed, as if he detected the noise coming from the woods, too, and Daniel, once again, had to re-evaluate the man still holding his arm. Those sounds should have been too quiet for a human to hear. There was more to Bradley Williams than was apparent, even to acute tiger senses.

"We're leaving now," Daniel said. "It would be best if you backed off."

Williams finally let go with a snarl. "You're a dead man. You messed with the wrong guy." He looked around Daniel and smiled at Sarah. "I'll call you, baby."

Daniel hoped the look he gave William told him if he went anywhere near Sarah again, he'd regret it.

Williams met his look without flinching. "You and I will be seeing each other soon."

Daniel bit his tongue. Every instinct, every fiber of his being, wanted to rip this man apart, to tear through flesh and bone until there was nothing left but bloody pieces. Only the feel of Sarah's warm skin in his hand kept him from acting—remembering he was here to save her from doing something rash.

"Don't call her again," he said through clenched teeth. Then he jerked Sarah into motion and stalked into the trees.

Along Came a Tiger (Tiger Shifters 2)
AVAILABLE NOW!

About The Author

Kat Simons earned her Ph.D in animal behavior, working with animals as diverse as dolphins and deer. She brought her experience and knowledge of biology to her paranormal romance fiction, where she delights in taking nature and turning it on its ear. After traveling the world, she now lives in New York City with her family. Kat is a stay-at-home mom and a full time writer.

For more on Kat and her future books:

Website: http://www.katsimons.com
Newsletter: http://eepurl.com/OxQQL

TITLES BY KAT SIMONS

Tiger Shifters Series

ONCE UPON A TIGER
ALONG CAME A TIGER
HERE THERE BE TIGERS
HER TIGER TO TAKE
TO TEMPT A TIGER
DOWN WILL COME TIGER

www.ingramcontent.com/pod-product-compliance
Lightning Source LLC
Chambersburg PA
CBHW051708180726

48283CB00004B/1260